THE BATH
SHORT STORY
AWARD
ANTHOLOGY
2015

THE BATH SHORT STORY AWARD ANTHOLOGY 2015

Compiled by
Jude Higgins, Jane Riekemann
and Anna Schlesinger

BROWN
DOG
BOOKS

Published under licence by Brown Dog Books and
The Self-Publishing Partnership
7 Green Park Station, Bath BA1 1JB

www.selfpublishingpartnership.co.uk

ISBN printed book: 978-1-78545-054-9
ISBN e-book: 978-1-78545-055-6

Cover design by Elinor Nash

Printed and bound by CPI Group (UK) Ltd, Croydon CR0 4YY

CONTENTS

INTRODUCTION

This year we received 1003 entries; many stories came from and were set in different parts of the world: South America, Wales, Croatia, Ireland, the Middle East, Israel, Malaysia, the Caribbean, Spain, the United States, Australia and Africa. And then there were 'local' stories: some in urban, coastal or other public places, others in domestic environments, even in cars...

Old age and death, the struggles within relationships, loss and separation popped up frequently as did stories of urban life, the destruction of the environment, memories of wartime, contemporary themes of poverty, displacement and survival. Writers were often inventive with titles, structure and language. Popular genres included literary fiction, magical realism, fairy stories, fables and crime; there was, however, less historical and science fiction.

The stories selected by our team of readers for the longlist of fifty and shortlist of ten made us think and, at times, informed us about various cultures, shocked us, moved us to tears or made us laugh. With compelling openings, clever endings and developed narratives, they either offered fresh angles on familiar themes or introduced new and challenging subject matter, written powerfully and with heart. This year's anthology includes the five winning and two commended stories with shortlist judge Carrie Kania's comments; the other stories, chosen from the shortlist and longlist, reflect the range of themes we received.

The short story continues to grow in popularity with readers and writers both nationally and internationally and now there are many more opportunities to find an audience. 'The Beautiful Thing', Kit de Waal's 2nd prize story from last year, was broadcast on BBC Radio 4 in March 2015 and radio remains one of the best media for sharing the genre. In June this year we attended the second London Short Story Festival www.lssf. co.uk, at which all aspects of the form were explored in dozens of classes. As we go to press, we are excited to be hosting a workshop in Bath in October with the LSSF co-founder Paul McVeigh paulmcveigh.com on writing 'That Killer First Page' – essential information for writers wanting to make their mark in a competition. And competitions still remain one of the best ways to get work noticed.

The 2016 Bath Short Story Award opens on November 1st, 2015 and will be judged by Mair Bosworth, a Bristol-based short story producer for BBC Radio 4. This will be the fourth award and we are proud to be part of the process in discovering new talent and providing another platform for more established writers. We hope you enjoy their stories.

Jude Higgins, Jane Riekemann and Anna Schlesinger
www.bathshortstoryaward.co.uk
Follow us on twitter @BathStoryAward.

Subscribe on the site to receive news and updates on the competition.

ACKNOWLEDGEMENTS

The Bath Short Story Award is a collaborative effort so where would be without our enthusiastic and committed team of readers? For the 2015 award we thank:

Mina Bancheva
Richard Cole
Fiona Longsdon
Nina MacPherson
Val Mote
Katharina Riekemann
Hannah Riekemann
Pat Robson

Another big thank you to Mr B's Emporium of Reading Delights, Bath www.mrbsemporium.com for donating the Local Prize. We also love to use Mr B's as a venue for our launches – not surprising as it was recently listed by *The Guardian* as one of the ten best bookshops in the world.

Writing Events Bath www.writingeventsbath.com continues to support and encourage writers at all levels and we thank Alex Wilson its co-founder for being the inspiration behind the Acorn

Award for an Unpublished Writer of Fiction and for sponsoring the prize.

In 2014 Elinor Nash www.elenash.com won the BSSA and designed all the artwork connected with it. We loved the cover so much that Elinor agreed to adapt it for this year's anthology and award, earning our grateful thanks.

2015 JUDGE
CARRIE KANIA

We were excited to welcome Carrie Kania, a literary agent with Conville & Walsh Literary Agency, as shortlist judge for the 2015 Bath Short Story Award. Before packing her bags and leaving the 'Bright Lights' to search for 'Brideshead', Carrie worked in US publishing for 15 years at Random House and HarperCollins. She was the SVP Publisher of Harper Perennial, where she looked after countless authors, including Michael Chabon, Barbara Kingsolver and Mary Karr. She loves debut fiction writers and will always be a champion of the short story. She works with Simon Van Booy, who won the Frank O'Connor award in 2009 for his collection of stories *Love Begins in Winter* and also represents short story writer and novelist Paul McVeigh whose debut novel *The Good Son* was launched this year.

She has taught at New York University, spoken at numerous writers' symposiums and is always happy to talk to writers at conferences, in classrooms and at festivals.

Carrie is the co-founder of the independent bookstore/ cocktail bar The Society Club in Soho, London, known for its full cocktail bar surrounded by books. The perfect mixer

– where writers are encouraged by Carrie to chat about their work.

Some comments from her shortlist report:

'The stories on this year's shortlist were of a high calibre – each able to bring its own individual style and, importantly, voice to the prose. When I read short stories, I look for trouble at the start, followed by a reason or solution. In the stories that made-up the Bath Short Story Award shortlist this year, trouble came in many forms, but I can't help but remark on the themes of the shortlist: love, death and growing-up. Sometimes all three, often two, always at least one. These are stories that deal with the way we live – in all corners of the world; diversity in action and emotion. Reading each story was akin to being transported into someone else's dream'

Carrie's comments on the commended and winning entries can be seen at the end of the authors' biographies. You can follow Carrie on Twitter @MissCarrieK

FIRST PRIZE
SAFIA MOORE

That Summer

That summer, I was sure someone would die. It wasn't a premonition since I couldn't predict who or when, more a hunch. Ivan reckoned too much sun had gone to my head, like those fellas in the films, hallucinating in the Sahara Desert. There was a steamy haze when you looked into the distance all right, but no mirages. Tar melted on the roads and stuck to the soles of our flip-flops. Ivan suggested putting them on our hands to climb walls, like human geckos.

'What's a gecko?' I asked.

He'd already turned away. I watched him make his tacky-footed way home. His Da didn't tolerate tardiness and Ivan had felt the sting of a belt on his backside more than once. I wished he could stay until teatime when the mothers started bellowing names, rounding us up like stray sheep, but he never did.

I yelled 'Fatso!' into the air in Ivan's general direction, but only because Noel Conway was strutting towards me like he owned the estate. I hoped Ivan hadn't heard. All I could see of him now were his head and shoulders off down the hill towards the real town where the shops, the bars, and the seven different churches were.

'Wanna see something?' Noel asked.

I straightened up, thrust my hands into the shallow pockets of my shorts, not quite squaring up to Noel's bulky frame, but I'd held my own in a scuffle with him once, and he'd never forgotten.

'See what?'

'Mrs Walsh topless.'

The Walshes were the only Catholic family in our red, white and blue North Down stronghold. There'd been no violence against them, although the possibility always hovered in the air. To most people, they were a curiosity, re-housed for their own safety. To others, an annoying itch, demanding the occasional scratch in the form of a low-level taunt. But to some, they were an alien presence who needed reminding of their outsider status. Cuckoos, to be kicked out of our cozy Protestant nest.

We cut around the back of the terrace, crouching so the old-aged pensioners in their bungalows wouldn't spot us. I could hear Mrs Snow clattering about in her scullery, her voice robust if a bit dodgy on the high notes of Shirley Bassey's 'Goldfinger'. When he kissed her, it's the kiss of death…

The Walsh's house was the end one, the biggest in the row. It had four bedrooms and fancy wood panelling under the picture window at the front. Mr Walsh had created privacy at the back with a slatted wooden fence, and a piece of hardboard hammered over the chicken wire on the gate. But Noel knew what he was doing. A knot in one of the planks had fallen out, or been poked out, and by hunkering down, we got an eyeful of Mrs Walsh sunbathing.

It was late afternoon, yet the sun's infernal rays felt like hundreds of hot pinpricks on the back of my neck. Noel stepped back and it was my turn. I recognized the cloying scent of the coconut sun oil my sisters used, but Mrs Walsh's body looked nothing like theirs, all curves instead of angles. She was lying on her stomach, reading a book, breasts unrestrained by the abandoned bikini top on the grass.

I decided to count to twenty and pack it in, but when I reached sixteen, Mrs Walsh rolled onto her side and sat up. She re-did her ponytail, sweeping wavy locks of auburn hair off her forehead and temples with long, scarlet nails. She reached for her bikini top, fastened it, and headed indoors. I stood up, stretched my arms and shoulders, feigning indifference.

'Well, wee man?' Noel grinned, showing the gap where Roland Hill had knocked out his tooth on the last day of school. Noel had been asking for it, taunting Roland, saying the weirdo in Old Hughie's Wood was his ma in the wedding dress she never wore because his da flitted. Mrs Hill wore too much make-up, had mice in her bee-hive, and idolized Marilyn Monroe, but Ivan and I had a different theory on the weirdo. It was a man, escaped from the asylum, in women's clothes and a wig. 'Well?' whispered Noel again. 'Whatcha' think? Double D?'

I hadn't a clue what he meant. Thankfully, I was saved by the horn. The three peeps of the water lorry that regulated our days like the knocking-off siren at the carpet factory, where our fathers worked. Except Mr Walsh. Nobody knew what he did, despite much speculation.

'My Ma'll kill me if I don't get the water,' I said. And I scooted off for the plastic containers every household relied on during the drought.

That summer, Kim McCaig and Phillip Davidson went missing near the end of the school holidays. The Twelfth of July had been and gone. Shiny-faced Orangemen in black suits and inappropriate bowler hats parading, chests stuck out with Presbyterian pride, and tipsy girls in hot-pants and unfamiliar tans dancing alongside. After the procession of bagpipes, accordions, flutes and deafening drums, there was a communal collapse in 'The Field'. Some old fella in a threadbare suit with too-short trousers acted the eejit, ranting on about the Battle of the Boyne. We are the survivors, my friends. No Surrender! I couldn't imagine the smell of fried onions and overcooked burgers in 1690, but we applauded him anyway, perhaps because he was still standing when so many were not. Kim and Phillip in matching outfits were tiny Union Jacks in motion, zig-zagging everywhere, hand in hand.

The day they disappeared, nobody panicked at first. Kids often wandered off, later found in some old lady's flat, tucking into ice-cream or stroking her cat. But when half an hour stretched to an hour and then some more, the two mothers lost it, went banging on doors and running down alleys. They sent us all searching. Ivan, Noel, Roland, and I went to the woods. Noel predicted Kim and Phillip were face down in the stream, drowned by the weirdo.

'They're maybe just kidnapped,' I said.

My guts lurched. This was it. Someone had to die that summer. Our search was haphazard and we found nothing. Back at the estate, two RUC men in bulletproof vests, revolvers holstered to their belts, were questioning people.

Phillip's ma was wailing, 'Oh, my God, Oh, my God.' She'd been the calmest earlier, but her fears had simmered, eventually boiling over as time made its slow, cruel progress. Kim's ma kept repeating the same thing to the knot of figures in the shade of her front garden, the only one with a decent tree. 'She's only three and he's only four.'

Mrs Walsh was at the edge of the group. She was beautiful up close, more sophisticated than the small-town mothers. Unlike them, she knew exactly how to look in an emergency. Probably had loads of practice in Belfast where the Troubles were. Phillip's ma cracked, screeched, and made to run towards the town. It was Mrs Walsh who stopped her, a protective arm around shoulders slumped like a defeated boxer's. Two heavy sobs from the pit of her stomach and Phillip's ma looked up into Mrs Walsh's face. There was a moment of recognition and confusion before she attempted to withdraw. She seemed on the brink of saying something terrible when someone yelled, 'Look!'

They ambled round the end of the terrace, hands clasped as ever, grins from ear to ear, sunlight bouncing off wispy blond hair. Kim and Phillip were back and they were completely naked. Unlike the scorching sun, time showed some mercy and froze. The air was heavy and oppressive, muffling every sound. Something metallic hit the concrete pavement. Mrs Walsh's chain belt, loosened from her mini dress as Phillip's ma had extracted herself from the unwelcome embrace. The two mothers ran to their children, enfolding them in bear hugs that looked unbreakable. All eyes stayed on them except mine. Mrs Walsh strode back to her house, chin unconvincingly up, and I picked up the chain that glistened like real gold. It was warm in my palm and I imagined my hand on Mrs Walsh's bare breast, her skin warm too, but soft and comforting. I pocketed my booty.

That summer, missing kids came home after sneaking down to the sweetshop for a gobstopper, or walking with pals for miles to see their granny's grave. That summer, we ran free and someone was always at home. Mothers didn't work, and didn't know the perils of putting tinned meat in stodgy, white bread sandwiches every day. That summer, no-one wore seatbelts.

Mrs Walsh was killed the same weekend Phillip and Kim turned up naked with no explanation, just giggles and shrugs. The gossipers said her husband got drunk on his birthday and gave her the car keys, though she'd only had a few driving lessons. She took the bend near the school too quickly and slammed into an oak tree in Old Hughie's Wood. Her husband survived but Mrs Walsh went through the windscreen.

They took her body back to Belfast for the funeral and next day her relatives came to clear out the house. I sat on our garden wall, waiting for something I'd recognize as hers to appear. Everything except the furniture was boxed up. When her brothers carried a white dressing table to the van, I saw her in the mirror, brushing her hair, squirting Chanel perfume behind each ear, and laughing, like she hadn't a care in the world.

I reached inside my pocket and pulled out the chain belt. Thirty-three links, the same number of years she'd lived, like Jesus. Over at the Davidsons' house, two slats on the Venetian blind parted, but only briefly. No-one came out of there or any other house. I held the chain at one end and twirled it round on top of the wall, making circle upon circle and slowly unravelling it again. A door slammed somewhere. I thought one of the women would appear to say some kind words to Mrs Walsh's family, bring them a tray with tall glasses of lemonade, the chink of ice cubes breaking the terrible, heat-hazed silence. But no.

The van's engine choked into action and the last man emerged from the front door at the Walshes'. He paused at the bottom of the path and looked up at the bedroom windows. Without the curtains, I could make out Teddy Bear wallpaper in one room and purple painted walls in the other. I didn't know anyone who'd ever gone in to play with the Walsh children. I wished I had.

Mrs Walsh's brother struggled to fasten the front gate. I slipped off the wall and ran towards him. He nearly knocked me over as he swung around.

'Hiya,' he said. 'Are you a friend of Martin's?'

'Not really,' I said. 'I found this. It's Mrs Walsh's.'

I dropped the gold chain into his big, calloused hand. It looked smaller, insignificant there. He paused, frowned. Maybe, when I said her name, it brought her back to life. Maybe, for a minute, he forgot the accident, imagined his sister just moving house, or emigrating to Canada or somewhere.

'Ah, I tell ya' what, you keep it. As a memento, like.'

He closed his hand around the chain as if he was changing his mind. He shut his eyes for a second, then cupped my hand and gave it back.

'Thanks,' I said, relieved.

He joined the others in the van, waved as they drove off. I saluted him, the only send-off for the Walshes. Grasping the chain tightly in my sweaty palm, I set off for Old Hughie's Wood to meet Ivan. He'd be waiting for me. It was that summer. There were trees to climb, a stream to jump, and hours to go before teatime.

Safia Moore is a former English teacher from Northern Ireland who now works as a writer, editor, reviewer and creative writing tutor. She has a PhD in Literature from the University of Ulster and has published flash fiction, short stories, reviews, and critical articles, with *Ether Books*, *The Incubator*, *Haverthorn Magazine*, and *The Honest Ulsterman*. Safia won the 2014 Abu Dhabi National Short Story Competition and views winning the 2015 Bath Short Story Award as her finest fiction writing achievement to date. She is working on a short story collection and two novels. Blog: www.topofthetent.com   Twitter: @ SafiaMoore

Carrie Kania commented:

'There are so many things to admire about 'That Summer'. It's a snapshot of boyhood curiosity. The narrator's voice perfectly captures the sense of a small town complete with its own secrets, prying neighbours, worries and tensions. With language true to the characters, yet mature enough for the readers, the author strikes a fine balance. "That summer, no-one wore seat belts" – one single line in the story shows how, in a few words, a whole season can be described. This story stayed with me.'

SECOND PRIZE
DAN POWELL

Dancing to the Shipping Forecast

And now the Shipping Forecast, issued by the Met Office on behalf of the Maritime and Coastguard Agency at 05:05 on Thursday 2nd January.

Wight:
South or southwest 6 to gale 8, occasionally severe gale 9 at first.

The wind shoves at the doors and windows and demands to be let in. It quakes the glass and howls when its entrance is denied, long ululant stretches of sound that raise Shadow's hackles and send her racing from room to room, barking in retaliation. I sit at the kitchen table, hand-sculpted from planks of ancient flotsam, and nurse another coffee. The phone rings. I do not answer it. It will not be him.

I curl on the sofa, Shadow beside me, as rain lashes the sides of the house and clatters across the roof tiles. The air inside, damp and salty even on a dry day, carries the tang of ozone.

Out beyond the slope of the eroded cliff-side, across the sand and pebble beach below, waves thrash the rock groynes and puny sea walls erected to defend the coastline from the wind and water that besiege it.

Beneath the window, a stain is growing in the plaster, dark and wet, and I stretch, reach out a hand and stroke the dampness forming there. The brickwork and pointing outside need attention. Sand and cement still sit in small sacks in the shed, waiting for him. The fire throws just enough light into the room for me to see the residue of white that coats my fingertips, the paint dampened to a paste by rain that trickles and squeezes through brick and timber to draw dark shapes where there were none.

In the distance, out across the shadowed sea, clouds collide, thunder mutters and grumbles. Shadow whimpers and I stroke her ears. I tell her it is okay, that the storm will pass, that the rain will fall until, finally, it has fallen, and then some other weather will take its place. Her brow wrinkles and a heavy huff blubbers from her flews as she nestles her body against mine. She sleeps and I strain to listen to her breathing beneath the rack and roil of the storm bearing down upon the house.

His house. Not mine. The house he brought me to. Invited me to stay. A cottage you would call it. That would likely be the best word. A cottage of indeterminate age. Stone and brick built. Sturdy. Its thick slate roof slathered with moss and muck. Years and years and years of wind and water have battered but not bowed this home huddled on a head of land that is slowly being devoured. One day the sea will swallow the very foundations of this place, will pull stone and brick and timber and glass down into its waves. One day. But not today. Not tonight. Tonight the storm outside is dying. Tonight the wind curls itself up. Tonight the rain passes over, sweeps inland and is gone.

Rough or very rough.

The phone rings and rings and rings. It is what wakes me. It is what drives me outside. I walk the path down to the beach, step from the pebbles to the sand, scan the roll of the waves. It is early and the hiss and shush of the trembling sea washes out all other sound. Shadow runs ahead and I follow her paw prints. She leaps the old timber groynes. I clamber behind her, stumble over the rocks arranged into fat grey fingers alongside. These structures are meant to protect the coast but seem to point out into the water like a warning.

Shadow keeps her head low and her muzzle swings this way and that, hoovering up scent, until she stops without warning and stiffens. Looking out to sea, she howls. The sound seems torn from her, not something she gives willingly. I crouch beside her, rub her flanks, but the howl spools out, relentless, unbroken. When finally it subsides, it leaves her panting, her jowls trembling. I cannot know that he was here but I am suddenly sure of it and stand and whirl, looking all about for some sign of him, his clothes piled in the natural windbreak of some rock formation perhaps, waiting for his return. But that would be too neat, too much like a story. And this is not a story. This is not. This is what is happening.

Back at the house the phone is still ringing. I pick up the receiver and say his name, say this is his phone, say it is me speaking. His sister is on the other end. She asks me how I am. I lie. There is silence on the line and then she asks again that I let her know, let his mother know, at once, if there is any news.

I nod at this then realise I must speak and so I say, I will, you know I will. You'll be the first to know, I say, the first. And she says, it's just that we've been calling and we worry when we can't reach you on the phone, we worry something has happened to you. And I want to scream, Something has happened to me. In my head I scream the words, send them thrashing against the surface of my skull. Something has happened to me. But I do not say anything.

You can stay in the house as long as you need, she says, as

long as you need.

I think of how long that might be. How long I might need to be here, under his roof, amongst his things, in his home, with his dog. How long might be long enough. I know it will be a longer time than they will give. If I were to stay until the waves swallowed the earth in which the foundations of this house are buried, it would not be long enough.

Rain or squally showers.

My leaving starts with another phone call. The sister again, calling to see how I am, how things are going. Eventually she asks the question; When do you think you might go home? I think about when he was still here, when we were here together and I think now what I thought then, that I am home. I don't say this to his sister. Instead I say, I don't know. Soon. There is a silence between us and for want of any more to say I repeat the word. Soon.

There is another silence, longer, broader, with harder edges, then she speaks the words I know she has been building up to for a while. The words I am sure his family has said many times in the nights since he was lost. It's just, she says and then she hesitates at the brink of it, hovers right at the edge of it before saying it anyway. It's just that the two of you weren't together that long. The silence that follows pulls my breath from me and I turn my mouth from the receiver. What was it? she says. Her voice is metallic and buzzes from the handset speaker. Three months?

I don't reply. Hello? she says. Are you still there? Hello? Hello? She calls my name and the crackling of her voice and the hiss of the speaker become a desperate radio transmission beamed across an incomprehensible distance.

Two months, three weeks, four days, fourteen hours and a few minutes. Two months, three weeks, four days, fourteen hours and a few minutes from first kiss to last. First kiss: outside the pub, huddled against the wind and sharing a cigarette, him with a smile almost too broad for his face, both of us leaning in, our bitter fag breath clouding between us. Last kiss: At the door of this place, him in his running gear, his lightweight rain jacket already glittering with drops, me wrapped in the duvet, Shadow bouncing at his heels eager to be gone and running, that smile bursting across his face again as he says, I won't be long, keep the bed warm.

Two months, three weeks, four days, fourteen hours and a few minutes. And now I've been here almost as long again. Almost longer.

I'm here, I say. I thought you'd gone, she says, thought you'd got cut off. No, I'm still here, I say. But you're right, I say, I should go home.

But I have no idea now where that might be.

Moderate or Poor

I pack quickly. Shadow flops herself down on the bed and does not take her eyes from me. The belongings I brought here do not amount to much and are soon collected from the corners of the cottage: a few changes of clothes, a handful of books, a phone, a toiletry bag, a battered laptop. Together they do not even half-fill the holdall I drag from under his bed.

I fill the remaining space with him; the crew neck jumper he left hanging on the back of his rocking chair, the smell of him faint but still lingering in the wool; a yellowed copy of Chekhov's letters in their original Russian, every margin annotated with furiously scribbled English, his attempt to speak across the miles and years that separated him from the author; the shirt he gave me to wear as a nightdress; a locked metal cash box from the top drawer of his desk. I do not open it and I leave behind the key, just take the box and whatever lies inside to keep it safe from prying eyes. I put his iPod, a first generation click wheel device he refused to upgrade, in my pocket. I find the letters I wrote to him, for years as just a friend, then for such a short while, as his lover. They lie in the drawer of his bedside table. Beside them sits a small, pale, cloth-covered box. I take both without hesitation.

Finished, I heft the bag to my shoulder and Shadow follows me downstairs. She squats on her haunches in the hall and waits for me to take her lead from the hook in the kitchen. I fasten my coat and turn up the collar against the drizzling sky. The door bangs shut behind us, tugged by the same wind that drags us down the path towards the beach. There is no going back. My key is on the mantelpiece, above the swept and empty fireplace. His mother and sister will let themselves in. They have keys of their own.

I let Shadow off the lead and she races ahead. At the same spot she stops again and howls. The beach is empty but for the pair of us. Grey waves slip back and forth, never quite reaching us, as if ashamed to approach. A flank of cloud obscures the sky. The holdall hangs heavy on my shoulder, tugs an ache into the muscles of my neck. In my coat pocket, the corners of the small cloth covered box poke through the fabric, jab at my side. I pull it out. The cream colour of the box becomes bone in the ashen light.

I could open it. I could. See the thing he bought. See how it might shine, even in the pallid morning light that barely filters through the cloud. I could. I could but there is no going back and so I throw the box and everything it might have contained into the colourless waves where it might be carried out to join him somehow. It might. But the tide is coming in and the box rises and falls, is lifted up and pulled down, over and over and over, until, finally, it is washed back to the sand and left at my feet. My heart thunders in my chest, the boom and crash of my blood drowns the sound of the sea. And then it is me who howls.

Dan Powell is a prize winning author of short fiction whose stories have appeared in the pages of *The Lonely Crowd*, *Carve*, *New Short Stories*, *Unthology* and *The Best British Short Storie*s. His debut collection of short fiction, *Looking Out Of Broken Windows* (Salt, 2014), was short listed for the Scott Prize and long listed for both the Frank O'Connor International Short Story Award and the Edge Hill Prize. He teaches part-time and is a First Story writer-in-residence. He procrastinates at danpowellfiction.com and on Twitter as @danpowfiction.

Carrie Kania commented:

'Loss hits hard in this story set against a crashing sea.
And, in many ways, water becomes as much a character in
'Dancing to the Shipping Forecast' as the narrator. What I
admired most about this story was the building tension and
the aching, specific timestamp of a relationship – reminding
us all that every second counts.'

THIRD PRIZE
ANGELA READMAN

The Woman of Letters

It is a perfectly ordinary morning, I have just told a young woman her lips are like strawberries in the snow. May strokes her bottom lip feeling for fruit, a sweetness that can bruise. She drags her chair to my computer, scraping the floorboards. The window is open. I listen to Robin outside, raking leaves - slow steady strokes.

'Tell him…Tell him…. something to make me sound clever,' May says, 'And ask, will I come there?'

I pull the keyboard to my breast. May licks her lips staring at the profile onscreen. It's my job to make her, all of them, sound ripe for picking by a man overseas. I am a woman of letters – the only woman for kilometres who reads and writes English. I heard someone call me an interpreter once, I didn't care for it. There's more of an art to it. I've married dozens of girls. Lives are moulded by the mouse in my palm.

I miss you, I type, I have never met a man that makes me feel… I click Send and skitter love across the world.

'What did I say to him? What's he saying?' May fiddles with a vest strap, collarbone like a lily leaf.

Onscreen, the man called Benji has replied. You look so hot in that new picture, I want to get you on all fours and… something that should not translate.

'He wishes you were here', I say, 'he needs you like air.'

I don't consider it a lie. Love needs a loose interpretation sometimes. I make the words of a 39 year old Canadian something a 22 year old village girl needs to hear.

May pulls cash from her denim bag. I count it discreetly, cataloguing the room as I see her out. It wouldn't be the first time I've discovered a small absence after a client leaves: coins, candles, a comb, a small bowl. The women who come here can pay half their income for a love letter. It's a small price for a dream.

'This one will marry me,' May says. Her footprints stain the rug by the door. Not everyone wipes their feet. They have nothing with colours that should remain untainted at home. On the porch, sunlight showers May's cheek with jasmine shadows like rain. I see a shadow on her cheekbone that won't wash away.

'What happened?' I ask.

'Oh, I fell.' May pats the bruise, laughs. It's a lovely lie.

I dash to the kitchen and bring sticky sweet dumplings for May's daughter. The child is four. I don't ask about the father. Every time I worry about her mother's lifestyle I procure a treat for the child. She's a solid looking girl.

'If I could afford it,' says May, 'I'd come tomorrow. I'd write to him every day.'

'Are you still working?' I shouldn't ask. I know she buses to the city on weekends, works, like so many local girls.

'I don't go to the hotels. Now someone loves me, I only smile for men to buy drinks in the bar.' Her laugh is weaponry.

Robin sits in the shade weaving a basket, braiding one

strand across another careful as hair. He sees May and blushes. I notice and my stomach aches. There's nothing my son can't make, except make a woman love him. He has been different since birth, almost childlike in his ways, but there's nothing childlike about the way he looks at my clients. Every night this keeps me awake.

May swirls at the gate and shouts, 'What was it Benji said, again?'

'One day, he will come,' I call, 'You'll live in his house by the lake, he says. Your lips look like strawberries in the snow.'

May skips like a heartbeat. There's a chance, I suppose, the Canadian will marry her someday. Perhaps not for the reasons she wants, but she does not have to know. Yet. For now, she only knows a man writes her love letters. That's what she calls it (love email does not feel the same.) And anything can happen. Tonight, she won't go to strange hotel rooms. She'll only dance in the bar. 'I have a boyfriend....my boyfriend wouldn't like me to...' she'll say. Boyfriend, boyfriend all night long, as if she invented the word.

Robin looks along the path, anticipating my next appointment. I sweep May's footprints off the rug like a woman made of dust. The rug is striped in shades of pink: blushes, rashes, bursts, furies of pink, as if the petals of a hundred flowers all blow to my door. Every day I sweep it and think of a Japanese man who, I read, followed falling cherry blossom to determine where to walk. The petals crackled, browned and dissolved. I don't know how he decided where to go after that. Everyone who comes here is lucky. I can advise a woman where love may lie, let her follow it to a life. I must do the same for my son.

'What day is it?' Robin asks over lunch. He sits on the floor, legs crossed, feet upturned as lotus leaves.

'It's Thursday.'

'Lily comes on Thursdays!'

He makes smiling look so simple I ache. I'll do anything to

keep it that way.

'Does she? I forgot.' I scoop rice to my lips, cover the lie with my bowl.

When he returns to the garden, I study Lily's dating profile online and click delete, delete, delete. The mailbox is clean. Outside, Robin fills the watering can. I fill the kettle. In separate places, so close by, we both pretend not to be waiting for Lily.

It's not only her he waits for, I know. He's waiting for someone to love, hold. His hair is short as the flock in a bean pod, and already receding before it has known a woman's fingers. If I could keep my son a boy forever, I would, to deny him the disappointment of love. But, of course, I cannot. I see he is a man, with needs I hate to admit. He deserves to be happy. It's my job to find him a wife.

I slice lemons, sprinkle tea into the pot and position the bowls. One is missing from the set. I can't imagine why anyone would steal one bowl, except, some girls just need something, I know. Lily wheels her bicycle up the path, careful not to damage any overhanging plants. The door's open. Through the bamboo curtain, slats of Robin's face brighten.

'Hello, Robin. Lovely lettuces! They've grown so much since last week!'

'Hello, Lily.' He clutches the watering can like the God of Rain.' His voice sounds as if he's been complimented on more than his crop. I wonder if he is lonely. Probably.

Lily props the bicycle against the house, steering the wheels so they don't scuff the paint. It's an admirable house, to someone like her, the kind she hopes someone will build her one day. There are bigger ones now, monuments of colour scattered along the dusty roadside. They look like doll's houses, Swiss chalets decorated with balconies and roofs that prove a point. Hungry girls wander past and say, Ooow. This one is beautiful. That girl from the village married a German businessman. He built it. One day I'll meet a handsome man from overseas …

The houses say, I am proof of one days.

The wind chimes on the porch shiver around Lily wiping her feet, hugging a folder to her ribs. I sit with a book like a learned woman, for that's what I am. That is all she sees.

'I can never sneak up on you,' Lily says, 'those chimes are as good as a dog!' No one gets close without their bark. I could have done with some when I was young!' She laughs like the wind chimes, shells bumping into one another all day long.

I don't ask her life story. I can't. I focus on what I must do for my son.

Lily sits sideways, legs dangling over the arm of a chair that was once fashionable. She places her folder on the table and pushes it across, desperate to get down to the business of love. I sprinkle sugar, squeeze lemon and discuss the weather. The ability to discuss sunshine when a lie must be told is something my husband left me, along with the English language, a son, and this house. I hear he married a Russian. I don't look at the pictures online.

'Here's my new photographs,' Lily says, 'what do you think?'

I leaf through photographs of her holding a parasol. Her dress is satin. Her face is snow, lips red, painted into a shape that never says no.

'No...No.... Definitely not, not this one, or this.' I flick the pictures away. Lily picks one up and stares at a version of herself that looks difficult to love.

'What's wrong with it?'

'You don't look beautiful,' I say, 'not enough.'

I hold another photo by the edges, fingertips leaving no prints. On it, Lily's trying not to smile. The painted backdrop is a temple. I imagine her living a century ago, attempting to fold her legs into the correct place of a chair, and failing.

'This one is acceptable, perhaps,' I say. 'But men scroll thousands of photographs a day...They'll always pick the beautiful ones. This photo's traditional at least, someone might like it, I suppose.' I sigh, 'If you were slighter…'

Lily nods as I sit at the computer. If anyone knows what people look for, it's me. I know what a successful man wants, if not how to make one stay. I scroll over Lily's profile. She peers over my shoulder, so close I feel her breath breeze over my ear.

'Does anyone want me?' She points to a small flag flying in the corner of the screen. A message. 'Who is he? What does he say?' She can barely stand still.

The photograph is of a man in a baseball cap of about forty. I silently read.

Hello, I saw your profile. I am looking for companionship. I have a son of five. Three years ago my wife died. I am lonely. I don't know how to be a single guy. I have a small house in New England and I work in design. I'm looking for someone to laugh and cry with.

I read aloud, 'Hello, I saw your profile. I am looking for fun. I've been married four times, never again! You look like you know how to give a guy a good time.'

Lily leans her head on her hand. 'That's all there is? Does no one decent want me?'

'Not today,' I say. Or last week, last month, or the one before. 'I'll change your photo, it could help.'

'Next week will be better, someone must want me,' Lily says.

Her voice is a question. She has little education, her mother is sick. She dreams of being able to afford medicine by marrying a man from overseas. She knows no other way.

'Don't hope too much. You're too old for most. There are prettier girls, sometimes it takes years.'

There are many things I could say about fate, men, and some things not being meant to be, but I don't. Not today. Lily counts money into my palm and walks to the door wondering how much love will cost, and how to pay her rent.

'If I don't find someone soon…' she says, 'I don't know…

I could go to the city and work in a bar. I could meet someone there.'

'Perhaps you should,' I agree.

I don't think she will. I can't see this shy girl coiling herself around tourists, demanding, 'Why don't you pick me? Buy me a drink. Take me home.' There's nothing bulletproof about her laugh, unlike May.

'I could go, just for a week or so, see if I meet someone. Then I'll come back, someone may have written me a love letter by then,' Lily says.

'Who knows?'

I shrug, it won't hurt for her look, come back disappointed, disgusted, and ready to hear what I have to propose. I hand Lily her folder and try not to picture the cloud coloured bruise under May's eye.

Robin is all eyes on Lily walking her bicycle along the path. He pulls a lettuce out of the ground and dusts off the dirt.

'Here, Lily.' The lettuce is his bouquet. It's the most he's ever given a girl.

Lily accepts it with thanks, sits the lettuce in the basket of her bicycle, drops of water blotting her folder.

I stand beside Robin staring at skinny trails of damp bicycle wheels on the path.

'I would marry her,' he says, 'if she'd let me.'

'I know, son,' I say, 'One day, we will ask her, sometimes these things take years.'

One day, that's all we are waiting for: Lily, Robin, and I. We wait for one dream to be fulfilled, be watered down, break, so another can begin.

Angela Readman's stories have won The Costa Short Story Award, and The National Flash Fiction Day Competition. They have been published in anthologies including *Unthology*, The Asham Award anthology, and The Bristol Short Story Prize. Her debut collection, *Don't Try This at Home* was published by And Other Stories in 2015. It recently won a Saboteur Award, and The Rubery Book Award. She is also a poet.

Carrie Kania commented:

'A translator's way with words helps women find 'love' in 'The Woman of Letters'. Editing hopes, she nevertheless – perhaps unrealistically – sets her ultimate matchmaking eye towards her son. Peppering the story with gorgeous metaphors ("lips are strawberries in the snow"), this was a story that transported me and left me with a dual sense of two kinds of dreams – the ones that can come true and the ones that will not.'

LOCAL PRIZE & COMMENDED
KM ELKES

The Three Kings

It was Friday night and our wages were paid – we were set for the dance down Kilburnie.

There were three of us – me, Francis and Robbie – living cheap in a flat above McAdams the butchers, where a yellow stink of fat pooled at the foot of the stairs.

I was chipping away time till the autumn, waiting to go to the city and university. Literature was my chosen subject – I had a poet's soul in all but decent words on a page.

Francis was a fast-talking savage who had little ambition, but reckoned himself ripe material for some sugar mammy from one of the big houses on the lip of town.

The youngest of us, Robbie, dreamed of great adventure (a motorcycle and a Asian girl were involved) but had settled for a hefty bag of skunk and a terrible paranoia when he heard the thud of McAdams' cleaver on his butcher block downstairs, divvying up corpses with a cheerful whistle.

We all worked up at the big hospital by day. Francis in the kitchens, though the Health and Safety should have known he was tempestuous around knives and spices. Robbie and me were porters on the wards, wheeling out the lame, the vacant and the cold – half of them having died, we reckoned, at the hands of those bandits in the kitchens.

It was sour work mostly and on Fridays we craved hot faces and full lips, nipples under dresses like night-time flower buds, slick-thighed girls.

Our routine was always the same. Back late from our shift, we thrashed up the stairs, undressing already, then flannelled hands, necks and bits below. We laid down a skim of deodorant and stolen cologne then began to dress, all the while the radio blaring hard tunes and us itching for the banter to start flying hot and thorny-sharp.

'I bet that crazy little redhead from the chippy will be there,' said Francis, because he was always willing to kick things off.

We piled up our replies, shouting over each other:

'If it's fish fingers you're after, Francis, there's some in the freezer.'

'Come on now Francis, what have we said about putting your manhood in a deep fat fryer.'

'So tell us, do you plan doing the business on clean sheets Francis, or just yesterday's newspaper?'

'I tell you lads,' said Francis when we'd had our fill. 'Your mothers will be dabbing tears when they find I've jointed you on McAdams' block.'

Ready at last, we downed a few stiffeners each and left. The dark, wet lanes shone with our laughter as we sauntered in, likely lads, rampagers, in clean white shirts and ringing shoes, all shifting hands and mouths.

It was a familiar route. Through the churchyard, where we tipped imaginary hats to Robbie's grandma. Over the old railway line, abandoned now to saplings and brambles, left at the corner by the piles of engine blocks that fronted Adair's garage. We passed the old Bakery and the Primrose Café, Elaine's hairdressers for the blue rinsers and the hard up. We ticked off each marker with a reverence that left us wet-mouthed with anticipation.

In truth, daytime Kilburnie was as drab as Vegas under sunshine, a mouth-breather of a town, a no-mark, Billy-no-mates place. But on Friday nights it kept the worst of things shadowed beneath broken street lamps and tarted up the rest, smelling cheap and good.

We reached the town hall, the concrete steps stippled with old gum and cigarette ends flattened under polished shoes and outrageous heels. The lads the kept the door knew us well enough and we strode straight in, flicking proud, invisible tails at the queue-bound lads, who looked on, taking bitter little sucks on their fags.

At the cloakroom, the pink-haired, tattooed girl gave us a wink and, knowing, let Robbie check his pockets five times before hanging up his coat.

'Are we ready?' I said and the others nodded. Then we pushed our way through the doors to the thick air of the dance floor, the heat of the thing.

'Breath it in lads,' I instructed. 'Get a lungful.'

We yowled and cried and settled in with early moves, swigging beer from cold-sweat bottles. We made believe we had night-vision goggles, x-ray specs that could sort out the girls who would. We were heat-seeking missiles, we held the nuclear codes.

Francis, like McAdams' dog licking his chops for a knucklebone, spotted the redhead from the chip shop. She was sipping something blue and in the half-light looked demure in a silk dress. He gave her the eye and she smiled. Francis moved in, lifting his chin for Robbie to act as wingman for the stick-thin girl with the overdone eyebrows, who clung to the redhead like a lifebuoy.

Alone, I scanned the floor awhile and in the corner saw a mystery, a girl dancing between the shadows and the strobes.

She was a little thing, despite the heels, with a bob that curled under sharp cheeks. She was bare-legged, dark-skinned, glint-eyed; wearing a short tartan skirt with some black lace affair on top. I had never seen her before. I had never seen the likes of her before. She danced cool, contained, as if she had a whole world within her and needed nothing else.

I put myself in a good spot, moved close and set my traps. She caught me looking, once, twice then waved me over. Taking the bottle from my hand, she sipped a sip then shaped into me, as though there had been a space that always needed filling.

She set to, plucking out my peacock feathers one by one, pressing the heft of herself into me, breathing hot words into my ears between songs.

We danced so long she had to take off her shoes, placing them side by side, neat as you like, under a chair. Barefoot she was feral, prowling and stalking round me until I broke, could stand it no more and led her through the fire doors for head-clearing air and a fumbled cigarette.

The night was summer smooth and we found a spot by the brick wall on two steel beer barrels.

Her name was Joy and she had an accent that came out in layers, something Eastern and Turkish and Scots. She seemed from every place, and nowhere.

'What you do?' she asked.

When I told her, she said: 'I never been in real hospital. It must be very much? All that sad and all that happy?'

'Yes,' I said. 'It's very much.'

Joy sat cross-legged, tucked stray hairs behind her ears and smiled as I played out my questions like a priest in a confessional. What had she done? Where was she from? Where was she going?

Some of what she said was treacled in so much accent I couldn't fathom it and some I never heard because every penny of me was centred on her lips, and the flicker of that tongue between.

She didn't remember much of school lessons – always moving on from one place, arriving at another. And yet all of them the same, she said. All those walls covered in pictures of homes and stick families with impossible smiles, Jesus on the cross, posters of times tables, the names of garden flowers. Always a map of the world.

She had travelled a lot, the names of the countries rarely stuck, though a few scenes were remembered: watching men race horses on a beach in a country so hot you took shade as crafty as any snake. There had been a city with cathedrals of glass, another place where the streets were so fat with traffic it felt like nothing moved for days.

'And what do you do now?' I asked.

She reached for my cigarette, took a drag and let the smoke idle out. Her black eyes glinted as she held my chin and drew me in, as divine and dangerous as a black hole.

When we kissed, I was delirious with strange notions, vibrating with extravagance and no little fear. The warmth of her rose through that dark lace and I thought I had discovered a secret, a tiny place in time where you can hide and never be found. I made plans for us with my lips still wet.

'I want dance with you some more,' she said.

But inside, some big, short lads had come about the place, smelling of engines. They had leather jackets, shaved heads eyes beady as foxes. They had fearsome smiles. Joy unclasped my hand.

'Who are these?' I asked.

'My people,' she said then pushed me away before they looked.

She went to the eldest (her brother, someone alleged) on tiptoe, head down, whispering something. Then they gathered, a black wedge, around her.

The DJ, Thin Tom, who was bald and lacked teeth but played some decent tunes, saw what was afoot and stopped the music. He was always a bugger for a bit of effect.

Francis came over, stood at my side: 'What's our move?'

The brother had a sullen lip, a hunched intent, a silvered scar on his offset nose. But still, this was Kilburnie, our place, our dance, and we were kings, were we not?

'Will we step up?' asked Robbie.

I saw Joy's shoes, scattered now, one upturned like an old, empty boat. And the powerful memory of how she had shucked them off gave me strength.

I walked over to them, all casual, kneeled and picked them up. Then turned for Joy made bold by the Hallelujah of her face. But the light in her black eyes was out and the brother blocked, pulsing in the lights like a wolf, lowering me with a hard gaze. One of his gang stepped out and took the shoes.

The brother unpocketed a tough hand and pulled Joy's face to his, then kissed each closed eye and looked at me again.

'Will we step up?' asked Robbie again, but too quickly and quietly, with no heart to it.

I felt suddenly bereft, the feeling of weak days as a young kid, flu-bound or fevered, watching cartoons on the TV and feeling far, far away from the familiar world.

The way her head was meek on his shoulder told me all I would ever need to know – that I was not part of her or them, nor ever could be.

They turned and left. She didn't look back.

Francis and Robbie pulled around me and we gave it an hour or two, shrugging and laughing, slugging beers and giving out hollow lines to familiar girls who knew our patter. But nothing would stick anymore.

In the end the lights came on and we saw the place for what it was – brutal, chipped and faded. That night we slunk back up the dark lanes to home, silent and weary as tail-lowered dogs.

When we got back to the flat, the downstairs door was ajar and the smell of butchered lamb all about the place. We counted out what the night had cost us then drifted away to our beds.

Even then I was plenty arrogant enough to think we could survive this, the three kings of Kilburnie. I was a boy, I suppose, still wondrous at how quick the change from found to lost. So that night I lay awake for hours, still as the dead, raking over the night just gone for some good excuse. I drifted off, finally, with a dream of Samson, and the woman who did for his hair.

KM Elkes is an author, journalist and travel writer from Bristol UK. Since starting to write fiction seriously in 2011, he has won the 2013 Fish Publishing Flash Fiction Prize, been shortlisted twice for the Bridport Prize and was one of the winners of the Aesthetica Creative Writing Award, 2014. He also won the Prolitzer Prize for Prose in 2014 and wrote a winning entry for the Labello Press International Short Story Prize, 2015. His work has also appeared in various anthologies and won prizes at *Words With Jam*, *Momaya Review*, *Lightship Publishing* and *Accenti* in Canada. Website kmelkes.co.uk_Twitter @ mysmalltales

Carrie Kania commented:

'A wonderful snapshot of a night out with the boys – the three kings of their town. Pitch-perfect dialogue and a cast of characters you'd likely see up on the big screen.'

THE ACORN AWARD FOR AN UNPUBLISHED WRITER OF FICTION
LUCY CORKHILL

Last Rites

Rose Cullen. Eighty-eight years of age. Two daughters, themselves pensioners: Violet and May. Three grandchildren; one great-grandchild. A marriage, mercifully short, to Charles. Forty eight years of widowhood. A handsome terraced house, 56 Firgrove Crescent, to go to her daughters upon her death. These are the facts of her life and she knows that they make her much like every other old woman, just part of the human slipstream. Rose sees this in the eyes of her carers, the girls who come to get her dressed and in and out of bed morning and evening, who deal with the effluvium of age.

A wet February afternoon, sky thickening with night already and Rose is dressed for a visit. Mauve skirt and matching cardigan over a grey blouse. Clothes the carers selected from the bedroom wardrobe now Rose doesn't bother with upstairs so much. Violet bustles into the front room, May in her wake. Rose goes to get up from her armchair, sits back down as a swab of Violet's rain-damp hair meets her cheek.

'Hi Mum. Oh for God's sake, you've still got the curtains open. It's dark out now, you know.' Violet walks across the stained carpet to draw them; the brisk movements of her arms making her raincoat hiss. Sometimes she doesn't take her coat off at all during a visit, as if to politely signify the intended brevity. May, taller than her sister and gangly, leans over to kiss Rose's cheek too.

Rose knows that this is the last time she will see her daughters. She is dying, very definitely dying. At night, her mind is a riddle of doors flung wide, the long dead walking through bold as brass. Mornings, she has a job getting the doors closed again in time for the carer's abrupt wake-up call.

'Mother, you're miles away!' Violet's voice, that edge of reproach. Violet, Rose's firstborn, alarmingly solemn even as a toddler.

'Sorry, dear.'

Violet goes back down the passage to the kitchen and May follows. Cupboards opening and closing, water running, the clink of tea things.

Someone came last night: Raymond, Rose's lover. Died in 1948 in a car accident; Rose hadn't been able to grieve, of course. A scream of pain, tears stifled in pillows. And then there he was last night, just as she remembered him, his face still a thing of stark beauty. It's time, he'd said. Held out a hand to her, and she'd felt that rush of being sucked away by him, swallowed by the great tsunami of desire.

Rose met Raymond in India when Charles was stationed out there in 1943. Heat, dust, dirt like she'd never known; Charles, pompous with medals flashing at his breast. Dull evenings in vast colonial ballrooms, ceiling fans sweeping overhead, waiters in white against brown skin, the mindless chatter of the officers' wives. Raymond's eyes suddenly on hers, the press of his uniform against her chiffoned breast, the movement of his body like a snake charmed from its basket. 'It's only a dance, pretend you're enjoying it.' Voice richly amused, lips against her ear. Their hands entwined.

Her daughters are arguing bitterly in the kitchen. Rose feels again the hope she has had, all their lives, that they will find some common ground. That they will become friends – perhaps a possibility in their old age. But it's not her problem now. She can but hope.

'It's the only option, can't you see that?' Violet is saying.

May, always the quieter of the two, murmurs something indistinct.

'If she wasn't completely doolally!' Violet retorts, her voice dangerous with anger. 'Don't make this so difficult, May!'

It had been easy to slip away with Raymond, go on one of the sight-seeing trips with a group of unsuspecting others. Charles busy as usual or maybe relieved to see the back of her. Varanasi, the oldest city in India. Climbing down off the train to the press of human bodies; Raymond's lost amongst them. Children pawing her cotton clothes – she'd worn trousers and a headscarf in an attempt to hide her femininity. Half-naked men with wild hair and eyes that did not meet hers. She followed the group down the winding alleyways to the great Mother Ganges, smoke and incense as thick as bread in her mouth.

'This is where they go to burn their dead,' Raymond speaking, suddenly beside her. 'The Hindus believe that if your ashes are scattered in the Ganges at Varanasi, you achieve moksha.'

Scorching heat, sweat and desire liquefying her. 'Moksha?'

'Instant release of the soul. No more death and rebirth through reincarnation.'

Bells jangling, hypnotic chanting, a wall of sound growing in intensity as they reached mountainous piles of ash on the banks of the river. Rose glanced around, saw that they had lost the rest of the group. Around her, Indians went about their rituals: sacred bathing in the brown water, long hair flicking jewels through the smoke-filled sky. Men hawking wood, their voices entangled in the babble of noise. The colour of saris like sunlight refracted through eyelids.

And then she saw it: a body wrapped in a shroud, feet and head visible, laid out on a stretcher of wood atop a huge pyre. An elderly woman, face slack in death, her family gathered round. They did not look like people at the funerals in England Rose had attended; muted grey faces gazing emptily at the hole in the ground as the casket was lowered. The dead woman's family were alight with something, dancing with light in the same way the little sacred offerings of flowers and candles moved across the Ganges' surface.

She sat beside Raymond on the steps of the ghat, their knees pressed close, when the fire under the body roared into life. Heard the body fizzing and spitting, smelled burning flesh. The same shaven-headed man who had lit the fire stepped forward – the eldest son, Raymond told her later – and then: the crack of the body's skull as he brought a bamboo stick down. To release the soul. A sound she will never forget. Raymond's hand found hers, but she was not afraid. She knew she had seen something raw and real – essential, maybe – and was filled with a wild desire to sing or dance or cry out, as the family circled the hungry fire, chanting, great flakes of ash raining down amongst them.

May comes in carrying the tea things, her face blotchy and pink. She puts the tray down on the occasional table, goes about pouring tea with the precision that defines her character. A meticulousness Rose fears held her back – she remembers May clutching her hand as a child, afraid to try things in case she failed, always in her big sister's shadow. A relief then that Charles had been stationed away from home for much of May's childhood; he wouldn't have tolerated her unease, would have forced her to do things that made her uncomfortable. Rose had coaxed and challenged her gently, pulling back when May seemed overwhelmed. As a mother, Rose has done her best.

If only there were a way to show her children, now, that everything will be alright.

But they must wait. They will come to know in time.

Violet brings in two chairs from the kitchen, and she and May perch on them while Rose's little television set flickers in the background: an antiques show.

'Mum, May and I would like you to have a look at this.' Violet is handing something onto her lap; the slippery gloss of a brochure. Rose's trembling hands do battle with it momentarily, grip it, bring it up to her face. *Nightingale Care Facility – personalised care with a difference.* She looks up, smiles. May is awkward, she can tell. This is Violet's decision, of course, and poor May doesn't know what else to do; because what can she do? Rose understands. Her role in this is to be quietly acquiescent. She would love to tell them that it doesn't matter, but she can't. So she makes an act of flicking through the brochure, nodding when Violet points out pictures of old faces laughing, a tree-lined garden. It certainly looks pleasant, not the worst place to die. But so quiet, so…dull. On death her corpse will be ferried from Nightingale Care Facility to the funeral parlour, to be embalmed for a burial in the wet English soil.

'It looks lovely,' Rose says, and both Violet and May smile.

That night in Varanasi sixty-eight years ago. Waiting until the woman she was sharing a room with in the Varanasi hotel had fallen asleep, forcing herself not to run down the darkened corridors to Raymond's room. Falling into his arms when he opened the door. Kissing like they were devouring one another, a wild hunger like nothing she had known before. Like they could swallow one another, be born again through each other. They had not slept; too much to say, to share, every part of each other's bodies to be explored. In the morning, she watched a smoky dawn caress the ancient city from the hotel window. Raymond came up behind her, laid his hands on her shoulders so her whole body seemed to be pulsing with the vibration of the chanting and the bells and his touch.

Those hands, his hands.

Rose shivers now to think of them.

Her legs were shaky as she boarded the train; the secret fires of her passion exploding within. Bite marks on her breasts, on her inner thigh, as if she had been roaming with wolves all night.

Back to Charles whom she had married in haste at the beginning of the war at her father's bidding. Charles, who raised his eyebrows when she spoke, as if a speaking wife were not something he had signed up for. Charles: solid, immutable where Raymond had been fluid. Dreams and emotions bounced off Charles, found no resonance in his being. When, aged fifty, he had died suddenly of a heart attack, he seemed more himself in death: the silent, cold rigidity of rigor mortis a perfect reflection, Rose thought, of his character.

And yet, when they came back to England in 1945, Rose knew that she would be alright. That she had seen something more than the sum parts of her small life. There were times when she touched upon it again: when she was birthing the girls, especially with Violet when she and the baby had spent a night dancing on the periphery of this life and the next, and Rose had heard herself make noises like the wolves criss-crossing her mind; or when May's mucus-shrouded body had been passed up through Rose's bloody legs. Or when she had nursed the babies; their eyes fierce with otherworldly communication as their mouths pulled at her breasts in the velvet stillness of the night.

The brochure is still in her lap. Violet and May have finished their tea. It seems even the television programme is coming to an end. Which means Rose has been drifting for some time;

May's expression is worried, Violet's frustrated. Doubtless they have tried to talk to her, and she has missed the opportunity to have a last, proper conversation. But then, what would they have spoken of?

Though it hurts a little to do so, she lifts her arm to encircle each of them when they kiss her goodbye. She tells them she loves them. 'I love you too, Mum,' May says, tears in her eyes. Violet squeezes her hand, glances quickly at May.

When they have gone into the February evening, Rose makes her slow, painstaking way up the stairs to fetch a bag she packed yesterday. In it, a few things: a simple nightdress, her address book, cash, passport. There are letters for May and Violet which she places on the bureau; almost the same content, but even Rose would have to admit May's is the more tender.

She has cancelled the carers tonight but rings again quickly to confirm the message got through. Then, carefully punching in the long number, she calls the guest house, Kashi Labh Mukti Bhawan, in Varanasi. Ashok Bhakar answers, his voice warm when he realises it is Rose. They have spoken several times in the last few weeks, working out the finer details: no doctors or medical treatment at the hostel, each guest must die within two weeks or they are required to make other arrangements. But Rose knows this won't be an issue, she is more than ready to go. Ashok has organised everything for her cremation for no small sum, but Rose doesn't mind paying for this last rite. His brother will meet her at Varanasi airport.

There is just time to go round the house, to turn out the lights on her old life. A car horn honks. She steps out into the wet night, locks the front door, slips the keys through the letterbox.

'The airport?' the driver asks, as he helps her into the leather seats of the taxi.

She nods, and soon the night is a blur of rain and streetlights speeding past her window.

Lucy Corkhill worked for ten years as a journalist while writing coffee-fuelled fiction late at night. She entered her first competition, the Bath Short Story Award, on a whim and was over the moon when 'Last Rites' won the Acorn Award. She's currently a full-time mum to her adopted son, working on her first novel whenever time allows, and running an illustration business. Inhabiting wild spaces makes her feel alive and inspires her creativity; she has lived on a 90 year old wooden boat, in a house in the woods, and in an off-grid cottage perched on the cliffs. She blogs about writing at www.livingtheedwardiandream.wordpress.com and tweets about books @lucycorkhill.

The BSSA judging team's comments:

'Last Rites' impressed us for the strong and original voice of the protagonist and an unusual slant to a traditional theme.

COMMENDED
EILEEN MERRIMAN

Hummingbird Heart

The lights on the medical ward had been dimmed. His eyes kept trying to close but then his pager would buzz, like a mosquito in his ear.

Mr Edwards chest pain ward 5... two IVs needed on ward 10...

Soon he would start to disintegrate, skin-bone-plasma. Perhaps, in the morning, the cleaners would just find a pager sitting in a puddle of primordial soup.

He was about to push the double doors open when he saw the label to his left. Mrs Turner. He had spent the last three nights trying to make her pee. The nurses were driving him crazy, ringing him every two hours to tell him that Mrs Turner's urine output was only twenty mils an hour. They didn't care about his crappy urine output. All he'd had to drink for the last seven hours was half a cup of coffee.

He hesitated, walked into her room. The woman lying in the bed looked like many of the other patients he had seen over the past three evenings. Redundant folds of pastel skin, limp grey hair, sour old-person scent.

He sank onto the closed lid of the commode beside her bed, ignoring the faint stench of expelled waste, and closed his eyes. Ghost-voices echoed in his head.

Low sodium – got pissed and fell over – are you listening, Tom, it's our anniversary today, don't tell me you forgot?

Something touched his knee. It felt like bones. He started, opened his eyes. Mrs Turner took her hand off his leg.

'Are you the doctor?'

'Um, no.' His hand bumped against his stethoscope. 'I mean yes. Sort of. Can I help you?'

Mrs Turner leaned towards him, her milky breath wafting into his nostrils. 'I don't want to be here.'

He blinked. 'Me neither.' He cast his eyes towards the room opposite, where a man had died earlier that evening. Perhaps he could steal into the empty room and resume his nap.

Mrs Turner frowned. 'You're just a baby. How old are you?'

He cleared his throat. 'Twenty-four.'

'Huh.' Mrs Turner pressed a button on the remote beside her bed. The overhead light flickered on, illuminating her narrow face. 'I'll tell you what I want,' she said, staring at him with eyes the colour of weak tea. 'I want to die.'

'Me too.' He put his hand to his forehead. Did I just say that? He didn't really want to die. He just didn't want to be awake. 'Um, what's the problem? Are you in pain?'

Mrs Turner threw her blankets back. Her sausage-like legs were oozing fluid, as if someone had just pricked them with a fork.

'Look at me. I'm old. My legs are so full of water I can hardly walk. I get pain in my chest every time I try to walk out of my front door.' She leaned forward. 'And, sometimes I don't know where I am. That's just about the scariest feeling in the world.'

He bit his lip. 'That does sound pretty scary.'

'I've lived my life,' she said, her voice trembling. 'My body's worn out.' She fingered the IV cannula sticking out of her left wrist. 'You can inject me through here. Put me to sleep, for good. What do you say?'

He shook his head. 'Euthanasia's illegal. You know that, right?'

Mrs Turner stared at him. 'You doctors think it's all about saving lives, don't you? That makes you feel good, doesn't it?'

'I don't know. Sometimes.' He glanced out of the window. The sky was lightening, blue-grey. The heart attacks would start rolling in soon, right when his energy was at its lowest ebb.

He stood up. 'Maybe it'll seem better in the morning.'

Mrs Turner's papery voice trailed after him. 'Just think about it, doctor. That's all I'm asking.'

That was Tuesday morning.

Tuesday night. The patients were lined up in Emergency like peas in a pod. Chest pain, query meningitis, confused, shortness of breath. Three nights to go, oh God, he wanted to slit his wrists.

The afternoon shift doctors smiled as they handed over. They were going home to bed. He had twisted in his sheets all day, too-hot-hungry-thirsty-did-I-get-the-drug-dose-right-what-if-that-kid-had-meningitis-after-all.

There was a black fog spreading through his head. He couldn't face listening to any more problems.

You don't listen to me anymore. I know you work long hours but you could try to be a little happier sometimes. Tom? Tom?

He gave the Query Meningitis a horse-dose of antibiotics and lined her up for a lumbar puncture, then took a rambling history from the Chest Pain.

Why can't you tell me when your chest pain started, or how long you're had it? It's your pain.

The ward started calling him. Pain relief – IV line on ward

3 – can you see this patient, she's not right.

What do you mean, not right?

I don't know. She's just… not right.

It was Mrs Turner. He listened to her failing heart, and her wheezy chest. He pressed on a sausage-leg with his thumb, and left an indentation behind. I was here, he thought, and was assailed by a new wave of melancholy.

He perched on the end of her bed. 'Have you got pain anywhere?'

Mrs Turner tapped her index finger against her head. 'In here.'

'I'll get the nurses to give you some pain relief, then.'

'It's not that sort of pain.' She slumped back against her pillows. 'Are you married?'

Tom shook his head. 'No. But, I've got a girlfriend.'

Where is this going, Tom? Maybe I'd like to get married, have some kids, even. Is that such a scary concept for you?

'My husband died last year.'

'I'm sorry to hear that.' He needed to go. He had three more patients to admit, a growing list of jobs. Still, he lingered.

'We never had any kids. Not for lack of trying, mind you. But we were blessed to have each other.' Mrs Turner tugged at the neck of her hospital-issue nightie. 'He gave me this.'

Tom swung the bedside light over, so it was shining on her upper chest. 'A tattoo,' he said, not bothering to hide his surprise. He squinted at the tiny winged shape, inked in green and blue and red. 'What kind of bird is it?'

'A hummingbird.' She smiled. 'Their feet are so tiny they can't walk on the ground. Did you know that?'

'I didn't know that.' He smiled back, felt a clearing in his head. 'It's beautiful.'

'I used to have little feet too. I was a ballet dancer, can you believe it?' She plucked at the folds of skin on her neck. 'Look at me now. Everything's loose and wobbly.' She fixed him with her tea-eyes. 'People. That's what life is about.'

'You can still be lonely,' he said. 'Even when you're surrounded by people.' His pager was buzzing. He turned it off.

Mrs Turner took his hand. 'You need to listen. You'll be amazed what you hear.'

Tom blinked. 'I listen.'

Mrs Turner squeezed his hand. 'No one ever asks me what I want. They just do things to me. I don't feel like this body even belongs to me anymore.'

Tom looked at her then, really looked at her. He looked at the delicate hummingbird, situated just below her clavicles. He looked at her once-tiny feet, now blown up like balloons.

He looked into her eyes. 'I think I can help you.'

The following evening he walked into the Emergency Department to find that there was only one patient to see, a service station worker who had been hit over the head with a cricket bat. His scalp had split open like an over-ripe grape.

'I didn't even see it coming,' the man said.

'I hope the police are after him,' Tom said, injecting local anaesthetic into the wound. 'Or her.'

He was just tying the last suture when the telephone operator paged him to tell him his girlfriend had called past to drop off his cell phone.

Tom charted some pain relief, walked around to the hospital reception to pick up his phone. It was sitting in an envelope, along with a note.

Thought you might need this. Also, your Mum wondered if you could call her if you get a chance. Michelle x.

Tom slumped against the wall. The telephone operator snapped her gum at him.

'You OK?'

'I'm fine,' he said, staring at his phone. It was still the third of November, for half an hour anyway.

He called his mother.

Then he walked up to the medical ward, his mother's words echoing in his ears.

You forgot, didn't you? Your father's only been dead two years, and you forgot.

Mrs Turner was gurgling when Tom walked into her room, like a blocked drain. Her bedside light was on, but her eyes were closed.

He sat in the chair beside her bed and tipped his head back against the wall. Someone was groaning down the corridor. The midnight melancholy was creeping up on him again.

Someone should ban doing seven night shifts in a row. I think I'm clinically depressed.

'Doctor Tom.'

Tom opened his eyes. Mrs Turner's chest was rising and falling, so fast.

He sat up. 'I thought I'd ch-check up on you,' he stammered.

'That's very good of you.' She stretched out an arm. In the insipid glow of the lamp he saw the bruises staining her skin, like ink blots.

'Did they take blood off you today?' He let her take his hand. Her fingers were very cold.

'Not today.'

'That's good.' He had torn up the blood test form before going home that morning. 'I crossed the antibiotics off your chart.'

'I'm so glad.' She closed her eyes. 'I had a dream today. About my husband. We were sailing around the Pacific Islands in our yacht, just like the old days. He called her Pukeko.'

'He must have liked birds.'

'He loved birds,' Mrs Turner said, her speech punctuated by rapid, bubbly intakes of breath. 'And children. He would have made a good father. Do you get on well with your father?'

'We got on very well,' Tom said haltingly.

I didn't forget, Mum. I just didn't want to remember. Does that make sense?

'And now?' Her breathing faded out, faded in.

'I'll light a candle for him,' Tom said. 'When I go home.'

'Ah,' Mrs Turner said. Then she didn't say anything else for a long time, and neither did he.

Eventually, his pager starting emitting a series of panicked beeps. It was a triple-7, a respiratory arrest. He ran down to the Emergency Department and blew air into a forty-year-old's stiff, asthmatic lungs with a bag and mask until the anaesthetist arrived.

The man died anyway, eight hours later.

Tom certified him dead. Then he went home and cried.

On Thursday night he admitted a steady stream of patients, until they turned into a big conglomerate in his head. Emphysema-heart-failure-pneumonia-heart-attack-ectopic-pregnancy-asthma-attack.

It was after six before he made it up to the medical ward. His legs felt as if they were full of sand. He thought about how in two hours' time he'd be driving home with the morning sun searing his eyeballs and the radio turned up high so he didn't fall asleep at the traffic lights. Michelle would have left for work, but he would climb into bed and inhale her trapped scent until he drifted into a dreamless sleep.

He thought Mrs Turner was dead at first. Then she took a deep, bubbly breath, and the seesaw motion of her chest started up again. He sat on the end of the bed, gazed out of the window. The first red light of dawn was bleeding into the sky.

'Doctor Tom.' Mrs Turner's voice sounded as if it was coming from very far away.

Tom looked back at her. 'How are you feeling?'

'My heart is going so fast,' she said, putting her hand to her breast.

Tom took his stethoscope out of his pocket, held it against

her chest.

'One hundred and eighty beats per minute,' he said, after a moment. 'That is fast.'

Mrs Turner's eyes shone at him. 'A hummingbird's heart beats up to twelve hundred times a minute,' she said. And in that moment he saw how beautiful she had been, and a space opened up inside his chest.

She coughed. 'How about you, doctor? How are you?'

'I'm OK,' Tom said, and realised, for the first time that week, that this was true. Perhaps he would take Michelle out for dinner tonight. Perhaps he'd even ask her to marry him.

Mrs Turner smiled, tipped her head back against the pillows. A pulse was fluttering at the base of her throat, and the hummingbird was clearly visible in the pink glow spilling over her chest. It looked as if it was about to spread its wings.

Tom took her hand. He watched as the pulse in her throat began to falter. He watched it until it stopped altogether. Then he leaned forward, and passed his hand over her eyes.

'Have a good flight, hummingbird,' he murmured.

Then he walked off the ward, out of the hospital, and into the day.

Eileen Merriman writes novels, short stories and flash fiction. Her work has been published in the *Sunday Star Times*, *Takahe*, *Headland* and *Flash Frontiers*, and is forthcoming in *Blue Fifth Review*. She was awarded third place in the 2014 NZ Sunday Star Times Short Story Competition, first place in the 2015 Franklin Writers Competition, and won the 2015 Flash Frontier Winter Writing Award. In 2015 she was awarded a mentorship through the New Zealand Society of Authors for work on her YA novel, *'Pieces of You'*.

Carrie Kania commented:

'A young doctor's exhausting rounds leads him to a brief encounter with a dying woman. The rush atmosphere of the ER is deftly balanced with the last breaths of life.'

COMMENDED
BARBARA WEEKS
The She-Wolves

On the first day of winter my father died. We left him where he fell in the pine wood, his body like a tree trunk, flat in the snow. We returned to the house, mother and I, dropped logs in the basket, stamped snow from our boots and shook it from our scarves. Mother hung the pot over the fire.

'He will feel the cold, do you think?' she said.

I did not reply. Neither death nor snow could make him any colder than he had been in life. He still had on his fur coat and hat; he would be warm enough until he reached hell.

She stirred the soup and stared into the flames, the wood damp and hissing.

And then we ate.

And then we slept.

And we did the same the next day and the next, as if nothing had changed, although we did not return to the pine wood where my father lay dead.

The following week Mrs Petrova came to the house. She stood in the doorway, her face inched by a chill wind, and offered us some of her bread. Mother called her in. Mrs Petrova put the bread on the table and warmed her hands over the spitting logs.

'Viktor not here today?' She always had an eye for him.

My mother sighed.

'Moscow,' she said, her voice a whisper so as not to reveal the lie.

Mrs Petrova nodded.

'Moscow,' she said, in agreement. Viktor was important. It was a place he might go.

And so it went; they ate bread, talked of snow, of Moscow, all the while my mother checking over her shoulder for my father's ghost.

The following week Ilya and Georgi Ivanov came to visit, talking behind their hands as they neared, like schoolboys, not grown men. They stepped inside, hats pulled from their heads and wrung between nervous hands.

'Would you like to warm yourselves?' I said and pointed to the fire.

'We haven't seen Viktor,' Ilya said, as they beat their arms to warm themselves.

'He travelled to Moscow, last week,' I said. 'He wanted to go before winter set in.'

'When will he come back, do you know?' they said.

My mother sighed.

'The snow,' she said, looking to the window, a flurry of white flakes in the half-light blurring the path to the trees; snow, the reason and answer for everything.

It had started on the first day of winter, the snow, falling from a grey sky, flakes soft and plentiful. Viktor, my father, had cursed the weather as he dragged my mother from the house toward the pine wood.

'Damned winter, damned snow, you want a fire, you want this, you want that...'

My mother tripped on her skirts, wet and torn, and I followed in their footsteps, deep in the fresh snowfall.

'Sorry Viktor, sorry Viktor,' she cried as he dragged her, his fat fingers tight in her hair. But he did not hear. He listened to no one. He wore his sable hat pulled down over his ears, to keep them warm he said, but it was so that he didn't have to listen to anyone. Too important.

'And that lazy daughter,' I heard him say, 'eats too much, talks too much, always complaining, you want a fire then *you* cut down the tree!'

As if that was all we needed to be warm.

A full fifty days passed. Icicles grew at the window and speared the frozen earth, smashing like glass as they fell. My mother would tremble at the sound and rush to look outside, for footprints in the snow, footprints of a ghost.

'Your father,' she said, 'he stored the wood... the woodshed...'

I said nothing. My father did many things in that woodshed but storing wood for winter was not one of them. Once, when my mother had been sick and shivering in her bed, with my sister who died before she took a breath, she'd sent me to the woodshed - 'get wood for the fire!' – as if stoking the meagre flames would bring the baby back to life. In the woodshed I'd seen my father, his arms wrapped around Zoya, the midwife. I had thought they were crying – for my mother, for the dead baby – but they began to kiss as if they could make fire with their lips.

And all the while my mother thought he was storing wood for winter!

'*I've* chopped the wood,' I said and put a log on the fire, sharp and hot, and warmed myself.

And I thought of my father, dead in the pine wood.

I thought of him and Zoya and Mrs Petrova, and wondered if he'd reached hell yet.

I counted endless winter days before they came to visit again – Georgi and Ilya, Mrs Petrova, Zoya and Uncle Konstantin and Aunt Dasha.

The deputation.

It was clearly a deputation.

A man like Viktor cannot disappear for the winter and not be missed.

Aunt Dasha and Mrs Petrova clucked and fussed like silly chickens and wrapped traitorous arms around my mother, who just sat and watched the snow fall, as if she had never seen it before, as if my father's hand still rested on her shoulder.

'Viktor,' they say, 'he has been away so long…Moscow…the snow…we have problems… Viktor sorts our problems...'

They have a list and they look to me.

To me!

As if I know what is to be done.

As if I know what has been done.

And I think of the time the Cossacks came and my father stood them down, in the square, hands on hips, beard dusted with ice. Everyone had run screaming to hide in the church, in stables, in barns. But he'd traded, bartered, earned himself a horse and a sable hat and coat. After, I'd crawled from beneath the table at Uncle Konstantin's and gone to look for him, found him behind the church where the Cossacks had left their horses. I saw him pat their steaming rumps, and then turn to Aunt Dasha, pat her fat rump and then pull her into his sable coat and laugh and kiss. I had wanted to run home, drag my mother from where she hid beneath the bed, with a baby held tight to her; my brother who lived only a few weeks. I had wanted to drag Uncle Konstantin from behind the bar where he poured the vodka that my father had bought for the Cossacks.

But I did not.

I did nothing.

We did nothing.

And now they stand before me, this deputation, and warm themselves beside *my* fire and look to *me*.

Because no one did anything.

No one.

Nothing.

Not until the snow came and my father dragged my mother by the hair in to the pine wood.

He had stopped when we reached a small clearing and pushed her, my mother, to the snow.

'You want a fire, take this!' He held out the axe to her and she took it as she got to her feet. She looked from the axe, with its long handle and heavy head, and then to my father and then to the trees.

'You have your axe,' he said, as he folded his arms and stood tall, 'you have your trees, what are you waiting for?'

And so she dragged the axe through the snow to the tree with the thinnest trunk.

'Not that one,' he was laughing now, 'that one!'

He pointed to a taller tree with a fatter trunk. I watched as she tried to lift the axe but the weight of it pulled her down. She was too small, too brittle. I went to her, took the axe and looked to my father. Spat in the snow.

'As if you could do any better,' he said as I steadied myself.

And so I chopped at the tree, the blunt head slow to mark the trunk.

'Come on!' he said, and so I chopped harder, and harder still.

'Useless,' he said. 'Stupid women!' And he stepped toward me, twisted the axe from my hand and pushed me to the ground.

Me!

54

In the snow!

I sat for a moment, cold and wet. My mother turned away, pretended not to have seen so that she would not have to come to me, else it make my father even more angry.

'Stupid women, stupid tree…' he said. On and on he went. He moved his hands up and down the axe handle and squinted to find the right spot on the trunk to cut. 'Stupid axe, stupid snow…' On and on until I gathered myself, got to my feet and grabbed at the axe, tried to take it from him. I pulled and pulled but he held tight and pulled back. We turned and spun in the snow, as if in a waltz. My father growled like a bear and I pulled and pulled and snarled and snapped and spat. I would show him, damn him! I would show him. I could take down a tree and split a log and cut kindle and make the tinder spark. I could do all that and boil the soup and bake the bread and stitch a coat and mend the roof and patch the walls and keep a house and I could set fire to snow if he would just let me have the axe!

I am not a stupid woman.

I am not a stupid daughter.

I am the one who survived!

Just give me the axe! I need to cut down the tree and have done with it.

Chop the wood!

Dry the wood!

Burn the wood!

Just give me the axe!

And so we turned and spun and I chopped and chopped and I heard my mother howl as I danced with my father in the snow.

And I chopped and chopped and howled with her.

It was a gentle thaw, snow dripped from the eaves, ice melted in the water barrels. And as it gathered pace so they came again, Ilya and Georgi Ivanov, rifles slung across their backs and a dead wolf on their cart. They placed the sodden, bloody fur of my father's sable hat on our table.

'The wolves must have got him,' they said.

I looked to my mother. If wolves wear skirts and scarves and take their prey with an axe, then it is true the wolves got him, I thought. She turned from the window, looked to the fire and went to stir the pot, his ghost gone. He must have reached hell; the devil would surely have been expecting him.

I said nothing to Georgi and Ilya.

And they just rubbed their hands to warm them, shook their heads.

'Moscow,' said Georgi, knowing it to be a lie.

'...Wolves...' Ilya said, knowing it to be a truth.

'The snow,' my mother said, the reason and answer for everything.

And so on the last day of winter we laid my father to his undeserved rest. They placed his sable coat and hat in a box – as that was all that was left of him they said – and buried it in the churchyard, the ground softening.

We returned to the house and shook the last of the winter snow from our boots and scarves. Georgi and Ilya dropped logs in the basket and brushed woods chips from their clothes. Uncle Konstantin left us a bottle of vodka. Above the fire the wolf skin dried in the smoky heat. It would make a warm hat and a pair of boots.

And then we ate.

And then we slept.

And we howled at the moon, mother and I, and waited for the snow to return.

Barbara Weeks' writing career began as a columnist for the now defunct '*Today*' newspaper. She later wrote copy for several other nationals before returning to education and completing an MA in Creative Writing. More recently, she has taught Literacy, ESOL and Creative Writing in community education. With a passion for history, and the short story form, she was runner up in the Jerwood Historical Short Story Competition in 2012 and Wells Festival of Literature Short Story Competition in 2013, as well as being longlisted and shortlisted in various others. In between writing short stories she is working on a novel; a murder mystery set during the Restoration.

Carrie Kania's comments:

'The first sentence of 'The She-Wolves' gives readers all they think they want to know – but the question that first sentence raises is why we read on. The language here allows readers their own emotional relationship with the narrator. And we are left hoping that after the thaw things end well.'

SHORTLISTED
SARA COLLINS
Lilith

We have nowhere else to go, so he puts me on all fours, like a cat, on the backseat. 'You're as jumpy as a cat and all,' he tells me. 'Stay still.'

The old Bentley's back window is filthy like always. The doors are locked. The amber beads of the rosary swing side to side from the mirror. *There's a trick to surviving it,* Lilith always says. *You need a quiet place in your head, wherever you can find some small-small bit of peace? Like the sea? You see yourself there, you hear the waves worrying up against the sand, but no-one else there, you hear me? Then, THEN!* – she always says, stopping to see if I'm paying attention, like I haven't heard this a thousand times before – *put him there and see yourself beating the mierda out of him, whack him till he can't feel his own fever, and make sure and kick some sand in his face when you walk away, you hear me!*

She always flings herself about snorting and laughing after she says this. Back where she comes from they called her *tortillera*. She likes girls, if she had a choice. But I don't love her that way. She was the first person I met in the Quarters, apart from the bosses. She was dancing in the empty bar out front, right leg hooked around the pole. She hung above me in a way that made me feel a little tug of something like worship. Left leg extended, her long body flashed in and out of sight, her head seemed to click into place on every turn. On the ground, first thing she asked was who brought me.

'He's my husband I think,' I told her.

Sundays are slow, so that's when Big Man visits. He's parked us at the dead end of Back Road, where no one will come, where he can take his time. The day is stealing away from us. Slices of light smear the wagging sign for Goodtimes Snacks and Groceries and the dusty pink headquarters of the RCFC football club. The shadows lie like dark ribs across the street, swelling and dipping like someone's breathing underneath.

I keep my eyes on the pale, plastic Jesus with prayered hands outside the Many Blessings Evangelical Church. He's battered and chipped in so many places it looks like he really has suffered and died the way they say he did. I imagine myself rolling out of here, pulled along on the cigarette cart, two middle fingers to Jesus and the rest of them.

Last night, Lilith and I took bottles of Prestige outside to cool off as we watched the sun slot itself into the sea. 'Night-tide,' she announced. The zinc roofs above us up the hill, behind the Quarters, past the main road, rolled and shook themselves at us, flapping and cracking in the dark. 'Cha!' she slapped at a mosquito under her arm.

'Forget carrying your water in a bucket and taking a crap in a bucket, bathing in a barrel. The thing I really can't stand is sleeping under a roof that sounds like a bus backfiring when it rains. First thing a bit of money gets you is a quiet roof.'

We sipped our beers, watched Antonio appear at the open front door of the Quarters, slip out of its dark mouth, cross the main road, and slide down the hill towards us in full flight, pushing through the macca bush as if he couldn't feel the thorns, his arms winged out on either side so that his white T-shirt billowed around him like laundry on a line.

'Tell me,' he said. His dark face seemed to slash through the moonlight. He had brought a small towel out with him, and he shook it out and wiped off one of our plastic chairs before sitting down.

'Nothing special,' Lilith replied. 'Just sitting here, waiting for tomorrow.'

I could feel his gaze bearing down on me. He never replied to Lilith, never seemed to see her.

After a spell, he said what he had worked himself down towards us to say. 'Hey. Doan' sit here and stare around so. It's bad for my business.'

He had the habit of spending all morning stretching and flexing in front of the cracked mirror above the toilet, making himself tourist ready. The afternoon saw him oiling up his long whip of a body down on the beach where he sold spliffs and coke to American women, white with heat and longing. They paid him to get them over their husbands.

'Cha. Your business done for today.'

'You doan' know yet what the night can drag in.'

I said nothing.

'You know, your ma shoulda made you go missing, like all those other girls. How you ended up −'

'It was my granny. My ma wasn't there.'

'Your granny couldn't have the sense God give a goat.'

'She just had more sense than was good for me.'

'What you mean?' he asked, but I didn't answer. 'If you poor around here, God help you if you good looking too. If a bigman take a set on you, you can't belong to yourself any more. A woman around here, I heard, the one with the sandal stall around by the Pelican, around there, sliced her girl's cheeks when she started −'

'No one cutting my cheeks!'

'It never work, anyway. When *that* bigman in their area notice the girl he decide he want her anyway, for spite. Another whole bunch go missing after that.'

'Anyway, if that was you calling me good looking, don't.' I started fiddling with a radio we had brought outside with us.

'You know you are,' he said quietly. His face was turned towards me and there was something mongoose like about the way he was pushing his nose in my direction, the way his eyes were so black and so bright in the straggling moonlight.

'When my sister Crystal went missing,' I blurted, 'it's then I knew those girls weren't really missing. That was year before last. I knew cause of how Granny went on, crying, flinging herself down in the front yard, yelling for Jesus. If she was really missing, Granny never would have carried on so. That was all for the neighbours. That's when I knew all those other girls couldn't really be missing either,' I said.

'And here you are,' Lilith said, but Antonio paid her no mind.

'And here I am,' I repeated.

'You can always count on family, eh?' Lilith said. 'I was going to –'

'You want me give you something to cast him off?' Antonio asked. He had taken a bundle of rolling papers and marijuana from his back pocket and was making a spliff, putting on a show of rolling and licking, with the focused slouch of all spliff-rolling boys.

'Ha!' I shook my head. 'I been here a year. That's twelve months of Sundays. You asking now?'

'Is the right time. Now. I feel something gonna happen tomorrow.' He was fidgeting, moving the finished spliff from hand to hand. He licked his lips once, then lit it. 'Yes, something must happen tomorrow but the question is, who it gonna happen to?'

'Leave that nonsense alone, obeah boy. She got to deal with

her Big Man in her own way, put away childish things, that voodoo included,' Lilith said.

'I don't believe anyway, in any kind of magic. Already put away childish things. I don't believe in anything,' I said.

'Pah! Children not supposed to throw off childish things.' Antonio passed the spliff. The ganja smoke crept into the space between us.

He looked up in the direction of the Quarters, up near the main road. A distant headlight threw light across his face as it swung the curve. The Quarters sat above us as if it had been carved from the mountain rock. He turned back to look at me. 'If I...'

Lilith snorted. 'None of you any use... You all the same... All the flippin' same. Even you, half in love with her and all.'

For a moment, she stood still, then she threw her head back and laughed and laughed until it seemed as if it was all rushing away from her: the whispering bushes, the mosquitoes, the clapping roofs, the ground beneath her feet, the night itself. Antonio just sat there, staring, shaking his head, holding the spliff, and I looked back at him while Lilith laughed and spun under the tin-can canopy, out from under the surprising weight of zinc.

The seat squeaks beneath me. There's a taste of rust in my mouth, a smell around us like burning rubber.

I pull a cigar from the box he has wedged between the front seats, fish around in his front pocket, but there's no cutter, so I snip the head with the coral handled scissors he keeps under his front seat and roll the body slowly between my fingers under his nose. They're a special brand the bosses bring back with them from Cuba, once a month when they're doing whatever they do there. Lilith says they're harvesting the next crop of girls who will pop up at the Quarters, *indocumentado* and confused.

'Light it,' he says.

'You joking? The windows are all closed up in here.'

He reaches around me, pushes the button.

'Light it for me, nah,' he repeats. It's a ritual. He always gets me to light his smokes, to rub his back with the organic coconut oil he likes or to pinch his earlobe between my thumb and forefinger while he falls asleep.

I light it, take a puff, wish it was a spliff, wish I could get *frass* right now. The car fills up quickly with smoke, in spite of the open window. I take another puff, quick before he takes it away.

'*Naughty* girl. Bad for you those.' He chuckles.

My attention is drifting out the window again, almost as if I *am* high. I'm moving around the car in slow motion, putting my hand on the sill of the open window. His fingers are puffy and dark. They fly over the buttons of his shirt. I say, 'I know this car like the back of my hand. I know it like the back of *your* hand.'

'I figure you do.'

'I seen you yesterday.'

He pauses. '*Saw*,' he says. 'I dunno what you're getting at.'

'I saw you. I saw you at the Hilton. I walked by. There was someone with you. Another girl.'

He doesn't answer.

I'm still looking out the window. 'You have a different girl now?'

'Girl –'

I'm playing with the scissors, guillotining the blades in and out so they glint in the advancing darkness.

'What's gotten into you today, girl?'

I turn to look at him.

'Who was it?'

He rests his head on the seat, closes his eyes. The blades slide together and apart.

I was scared in the beginning, that first day, I was nothing but a silly young girl, but what no-one told me, what I'm telling you now, is that the most terrifying thing is that it becomes easy after a while.

'You know,' I say, turning to look at him, working the blades in my right hand, 'you couldn't really believe in all of that' – I nod my head towards the swinging rosary, catch a glimpse of myself in the mirror as I do. Thin, ragged, with eyes that look like they're trying to escape my face.

'How you mean?' His eyes are open again, watchful.

'That. Always hanging there. What it's about. The sacrifice. Not just Jesus either. I mean you have to sacrifice *yourself* to it as well. So far the only thing I ever seen you sacrifice is me. So I have to figure you don't believe in it.'

He shakes his head. 'This must be what they meant,' he mutters. 'I would have been better off leaving you alone.'

Next thing I know, the scissors, with a sudden appetite for blood, leap in my hand. One of the blades slices my palm, up to my thumb.

'Is only a nick,' I tell him. 'I can see you're worried.'

'Girl, can you stop clicking those things. It's driving me crazy…'

He's pushing himself further away from me on the seat now. His eyes are like soft-boiled eggs floating in water. Although he doesn't seem to know it, Lilith is there, in the front seat. *This car is a shithole*, she says. I know. She says that I must tell him that what love requires, above all else, is truth. I imagine how he must see me now, rising above him, carved out of night, smiling, smiling, always smiling. Sweat falling from my face onto his forehead. I'm filled with a heat that leaves my arms and legs numb. There's no greater love than this.

'*This* is sacrifice,' I say.

Sara Collins was born in Jamaica and grew up in the Cayman Islands. She now divides her time between Cayman and London. After studying law at LSE, she worked as a lawyer for seventeen years and was a partner in various law firms. She decided recently to pursue a career as a full time writer and is delighted to have been shortlisted for the Bath Short Story Award. Sara's work has also been published in *The Caribbean Writer.* She is studying for the MSt in Creative Writing at Cambridge University and working on her first novel.

SHORTLISTED
SOPHIE HAMPTON
Boy Uncharted

One evening, Bezier's mother tells him that there are canals on Mars. She has seen a picture; it was in a magazine left in the launderette where she operates the dry cleaning machine and does the service washes and the ironing. Bezier thinks that men must have been to Mars as well as to the moon. He now has three planets on which to search for his father. Bezier does not sleep well. He listens to the warm south-easterly wind, *le vent du diable*, which has been known to drive humans and animals insane, whip itself into a fury.

His mother creeps into his room, 'Are you awake?' she says. 'I want to show you something.'

He is relieved when she opens the shutters because the wind blows the scent of jasmine from the balcony and masks the alcohol on her breath. In a break in the cloud, the moon gleams full and bright. It illuminates the perspiration on his mother's forehead and the ladder of scars on her pale, plump arms.

'Look,' she says. 'It's Mars!'

Bezier stares at the ball in the sky: the moon has spawned a small blood-coloured version of itself.

The next day, in the playground, a girl asks Bezier if his father is in prison.

'Papa works on Mars,' he says. 'It's too far to come home very often.'

The girl narrows her eyes. 'What does he do?'

'He works on a barge on the canals.'

She skips away. Her hair flies in the wind.

The laughter in the playground crescendos and children flock towards Bezier like pigeons to the old women who scatter bread in the park. Bezier thinks that he might be sick. He has said something stupid. He knows that he is stupid. He is good at counting and he loves maps but he is two years older than the boys and girls in his class, and his mother calls him *my little idiot*.

'Hey,' someone shouts. Bezier turns. A mouthful of phlegm hits his face. He wipes his eyes and a punch in the stomach floors him. A girl kicks his shin, in the spot where a bruise has just faded from purple to green. All he can see is shoes: steel toe-caps, yellowed plimsoles, scuffed leather. When the girl kicks him again she screeches and clutches her arm. She has been stung by a bee. She runs across the playground and the crowd follows.

When Bezier arrives home – one thousand two hundred and thirty-four paces (counted as twelve times one hundred add thirty-four) from his school to the block, and forty-eight steps up to the third floor apartment – his mother is asleep on the sofa. Her lips, slightly parted, are stained the colour of blackberries. A new blot has formed on the velour, under the neck of the wine bottle that lies beside her. A sprinkling of cigarette ash looks like moon dust. Bezier goes to the bathroom and stands on tiptoe in front of the mirror. His ear is swollen and his cheek is cut. He tries to wash the blood out of his shirt with a fat block of soap, which slips again and again from his fingers.

He stands next to his mother and watches her chest rise and fall; her blouse is speckled with blue and white flecks of washing powder. 'Why did you tell me there were canals on Mars?' he whispers. He wonders if she knew that he would repeat it at school. He kneels next to the sofa. His mother's skirt has bunched up around her thighs to reveal silvery stretch marks and clusters of thin purple veins.

'Maman,' he says.

She opens her eyes.

'Maman, is Papa in prison?'

She lies still for a few moments and turns onto her side. 'Leave me alone. I started work at six.' She yawns; fillings checker her teeth like a chessboard.

'Is Papa in prison?'

'Shut up!' She props herself against the arm of the sofa and straightens her skirt. She puts the wine bottle to her mouth, 'Shit,' she says and drops it. It bounces on the parquet and rolls under the sideboard. 'Open another one.'

Bezier takes a bottle from the rack. When he twists the corkscrew his grazed palm stings. He opens the cupboard to find a glass. 'Just give me the bottle,' says his mother. She studies him through bloodshot eyes. 'What happened to your face? Have you been fighting?'

'A girl asked if Papa was in prison.'

'What did you say?'

'I said he worked on Mars.'

She snorts. 'My little idiot. My God your father must have been stupid.'

Bezier stares at his feet, as he does when he wants to ask about his father but doesn't. A squall crashes the shutters against the windows and blows a flurry of questions from Bezier's mouth: 'Where is Papa? What does he do? Why doesn't he want to see us? Why don't you ever talk about him?' His heart beats fast.

His mother drinks from the wine bottle as Bezier might drink from a bottle of milk.

'I met your father in a bar,' she says, finally. 'I was on holiday in Béziers, during the *feria*. He was a matador. He was standing on a table and when he held the bull's ear above his head and looked round the room, he caught my eye. I was beautiful until you were born.' She lights a cigarette, inhales. 'He killed a bull and made a boy that night, my little idiot.' She laughs, so hard that her hand shakes and wine slops onto the sofa.

Bezier does not think that killing an animal is funny. He does not understand what his mother means about the boy. Her laugh reminds him of a cock's cry and chalk on a blackboard.

'What's Papa's name?'

His mother closes her eyes.

'Maman?'

His father could be on another planet and Bezier does not even know his name. He shuts the door quietly. He stands in the corridor and studies a painting on the wall: in the background, the sky glows orange and yellow; in the bullring, the matador wears red and gold. The bull's face is shielded by the matador's cape but barbed spears pierce its neck and its hide is matted with blood.

Bezier cannot sleep. Shutters bang and dogs howl and the wind streaks through the trees. He thinks of the expression on the matador's face; it is cruel and hard, like his mother's.

On Saturdays and after school if his mother is working the late shift, Bezier helps in the launderette. As he grows plump and pale, his classmates – lean and brown as conkers – play football or tag under a fierce sun, which never seems to set. Bezier likes the launderette in winter but in summer his hair sticks to his neck and he has to change the flypaper every day and the soiled washing reeks of sweat. He holds his breath as he checks the pockets: he finds receipts and used handkerchiefs and occasionally a few *centimes*, which he slips into his shoe. When a wash finishes, he transfers the laundry into a tumble dryer and after it dries he bundles it into a basket, which he leaves outside the room, at the back for his mother to steam press or iron.

Bezier isn't allowed into the room at the back, nor are the customers; men go in with deliveries or with maintenance to do. Bezier has only seen the room once. His mother didn't hear him come in over the hum and click of the dry cleaning machine and the whirr and creak of the fan. She stood in front of a mirror, tall in heels, painting her lips. She had changed from her apron and trousers into a green dress that Bezier had never seen; the zip at the back was open and she wasn't wearing a bra.

Bezier's breaths were fast and shallow. The fumes from the solvent made him light-headed. 'Maman', he said.

She started and turned. 'How dare you come in!' She kicked the flat shoes on the floor under the chaise longue and took a cushion and plumped it as though she hated it. 'Come here,' she said and sat down. 'Do up my zip.'

Bezier lifted her hair. His hands trembled and he caught her skin between the zip's metal teeth.

'Ow!' she said. 'Is it bleeding?'

'No,' said Bezier. He began to cry. Through his tears, the dashes of blood looked like a trail of red ants crawling up his mother's spine. When he wiped his nose he could smell her violet scent on his fingers.

She put the lipstick in a vanity case. She turned on the radio and switched off the fluorescent lights so that only a stand lamp in the corner lit the room. The pressed clothes hanging from the rails shivered in the fan's breeze.

'Stop sniffing,' she said, 'and get out. The fumes aren't good for you.'

As Bezier waits for a wash to finish, he sits on the bench and stares at the faded map of France on the wall. He can recite all ninety-six *departments* with his eyes shut: *Ain, Aisne, Allier…* but today he is tired and stops at *Bouches-du-Rhone.* Zips and buttons clunk and thud as they roll in the drum. A red garment swishes in and out of sight behind the glass door, like a matador's cape whipped in front of a bull. He stands up and searches for Béziers on the map. He finds it next to the Mediterranean and hopes that one day he will be able to visit the sea.

'Number four's finished,' his mother says. She hands Bezier a couple of tokens for the tumble drier and goes outside. He watches her through the window. She cups her hand around a cigarette as she tries to light it. Leaves and litter swirl around her ankles.

Bezier bundles an armful of sheets into the drier. When he starts the machine he thinks that something is wrong with the motor but realises that the buzzing comes from a bee that has flown into the launderette. Each time it hits a wall or the window it makes a dull thwack and Bezier worries that it will join the graveyard of flies on the sticky paper. He tries to guide the bee to the door but it flies out of reach. He sits down and the bee circles his head before landing on his arm. He peers at its black and yellow hair and its segmented legs and the veins in its translucent wings. He gently touches the hair with his forefinger; the bee quivers.

His mother comes back in and the bee rises, its wings whirring like a helicopter's blades. She flails her arms and grabs a magazine and swats the insect. 'A bee sting can kill,' she says, as she goes into the room at the back.

At five to seven, as Bezier scrapes congealed soap out of the powder trays, Serge, the launderette owner, arrives to cash-up. He turns the sign on the front door to *FERME.*

'Off you go,' he says. 'Your mother won't be long.'

Bezier stops at the *tabac* – twenty paces from the launderette

– to buy sweets with the *centimes* he has in his shoe. He arrives home – three hundred and forty paces from the *tabac* to the block and forty-eight steps up to the third floor apartment. He goes onto the balcony where he checks that the bee is still in his pocket. He uses his fingers to dig a hole in the earth in a window box. He wonders where his father, the matador, buried the bull.

He places the bee on his palm; it is weightless. It has lost a wing and three legs. He cups his hand to drop the insect into its grave but a swirl of wind takes it up, up, up into the sky.

When the grandfather clock heaves its hands to seven-thirty, Bezier spoons the contents of a jar of cassoulet into a pan. He lays the table: placemats, cutlery and glasses for two. He heats the stew until it bubbles. He serves half onto his plate. He eats alone.

Bezier listens out for the sound of keys in the door as he leans over the balcony railings. The moon is full and bright but the red planet is no longer visible. The wind has dropped and the trees are still. In the block opposite, squares of light from a hundred windows frame the silhouettes of unknown fathers.

Sophie Hampton has had her fiction broadcast on BBC Radio 4 and in publications including *Southword*, *The London Magazine*, *The Bristol Short Story Prize Anthology*, *The View From Here*, *The Yellow Room,* the *Eastern Daily Press and The Bath Short Story Award Anthology 2014.* She has won competitions including the Sean O'Faolain International Short Story Prize and *The London Magazine* Short Story Competition. She was awarded 2nd Prize at the Wells Festival of Literature and has been shortlisted for Bridport, Bristol and Fish. Sophie has an MA Writing (Distinction) from Sheffield Hallam University and starts a PhD in Creative and Critical Writing at UEA in October 2015.

SHORTLISTED
EMMA SEAMAN

The Ends of the Earth

'I've wanted to do this for years,' my father tells me. 'It's top of my bucket list.'

I didn't know he had a bucket list, or needed one; but I can hear he's proud of himself for knowing the term.
'It's an amazing spectacle, something to tell the grandchildren,' he says, 'So I thought - why not bring them along, make a holiday to remember? '
Dragging my boys away from X-boxes and Wi-Fi and playdates? Yes, that will be a holiday they'll remember, for all the wrong reasons.

I hold out for as long as I can. Give excuses about the distance, travel sickness, money. Until my father offers to pay, even books our tickets, so all I have to do is pack and turn up at the station; the decision taken out of my hands, like so much else. We never mention the real reason for my reluctance, his insistence, but let it float between us, unspoken and unspeakable. At the other end, my sister picks us up from the station, the first I've seen of her for too many months. I let myself be hugged and she pulls back to look into my eyes. She tries to talk to me as she drives, to probe my pain level, but the boys are fractious, and as the miles grind past her forehead corrugates with frustration.

At our rented cottage, the children explode from the car, then tear from room to room discovering the limits of their new space. I drop my bags by the window and stare out at the slate sea; this isn't a beach resort, just a place where the land runs out, the tattered edge of the world. My father returns from reconnaissance across the dunes, buoyed by clear skies and pure air.

'The timing is superb,' he confides with shining eyes. 'There have been massive disturbances in the ionosphere – solar flares, to you and me. After forty hours those supercharged particles will hit the earth's atmosphere – and boom!'

His hands describe a huge arch in the sky, and his smile arcs in mirror-image beneath.

There are no husbands here. My sister's is absent because he couldn't get a week's leave at such short notice. Mine is working abroad again, this time for good. The boys don't seem to have noticed his glacial drift away from us, working ever-longer hours, and even when he was home, the unbroachable silence. I will have to sit down and have the dreaded conversation with them soon.

'I don't want to uproot the boys,' he'd said, expecting me to applaud his generosity. 'Besides, I need a base when I'm back in this country.'

I wanted to hit him, for the neat way he was bundling us up like mismatched china, packing us neatly to one side. I wanted to pour paint on his car, shred the crotches of his suits. But he wouldn't have stayed around to see it. And I would have had to clear up the mess.

'I'll make sure there's as little disruption to their lives as possible,' he told me, and I knew then he'd been planning this for months. 'This surely can't come as a surprise?' he added. No, but it was still a shock. I stood to one side, arms tight-banded across my chest, watching him pack; knowing it would be the last time, and feeling the trite resonance of it. He gave an impatient shrug, that timeworn, too familiar gesture.
'Stop watching me,' he said. 'Always bloody taking notes. Haven't you got anything better to do?'

I've always preferred to observe. I remember travelling with my parents, staring out of the car windows, trying to burn each sensation onto my memory. I inhaled sweet cow parsley foaming white in the hedgerows, bobbing and ducking in the car's slipstream; watched an orange harvest moon rise over the dark hills, molten and swollen as wax in a lava lamp. As we sped through each town, I peered into windows glowing yellow in the dusk, curtains not yet drawn across the stage, desperate for a glimpse into other lives. I yearned for those lives that would go on, even though I had passed by.

I sleep better here, and rise late after rolling in the shallow dreams that come just before waking, where everything is vivid and makes some kind of sense. During the day, the tablets that hold me on the fabled even keel keep me from feeling anything at all, but on the soft frayed edge between sleeping and waking, my resistance slips. I slide between the cracks, falling into places where reality is worn thin and smooth, searching for another existence. I can't control those glimpses of other realities, can't force them to appear, though I've tried. They are fragile, willfully elusive, and retreat if I reach for them directly.

I slipped, just for a moment, at the railway station as we waited to board. There was a girl there, getting off the train with her family. She was about the same age as my eldest boy, a pale skinny child with a careless flick of freckles across her small nose. She gazed at me with a thousand-yard stare, as if she recognised me as her own and saw some truth that I had hidden, even from myself. My boys don't have freckles. Why would they? But sometimes, the children I see in my head... I looked at the boys and wondered whose they really were, how they came about. It happens too often, this sense that I've fallen into someone else's life.

There are no routines here, and that in itself is a holiday. I've been dragging myself through the grind of each day, barely existing. We eat at haphazard times, take fresh air and exercise as if they are medicine. Boys, I have long suspected, are like dogs; manageable, even adorable, as long as you walk them once a day and burn off their energy. They race ahead of me down the beach, chasing my father who bounds like the biggest puppy of them all. He likes it this way, just his flesh and blood, his children and my children.

I hunch into my fleece to keep out the chills and watch my sister crunching through the brown sugar sand, suede boots a careful distance from the water line.
'Do you ever sense there's another life you should have lived?' I ask her. 'That somewhere a version of you is living another life?'
She shakes her head, shrugs slim shoulders in her down-filled jacket.
'It's understandable to wish things had turned out differently,' she says, trying to medicate me with professional calm. I am grimly pleased that the biting cold makes my exasperation visible as a plume of dragon's breath.

'It's not about wishing things were different, but actually seeing glimpses of other lives,' I tell her, but she shakes her head, crisp blonde waves breaking around her face.

'Don't you ever feel that if you turn a corner, you'll find everything's different?' I ask urgently. 'I'm not talking about the big events, they're the ones you wish you could change, but they're fixed points, inevitable. It's the subtle things that catch you out...'

'It will be okay,' she replies, as if by saying those words she can make it so. 'What happened to you and the boys is wrong. But it's not the end of the world;
you have to think of it as the start of a new chapter.'

I resent her crappy New Age mantras and walk more quickly. She thinks I don't believe her but I simply can't summon up the energy to explain. It's quite common to think you already know a place you've never visited before. One hemisphere of the brain works fractionally faster than the other, and that infinitesimal, split-second time-lag gives you a moment of temporal dislocation. But the flashes I get are more than déja vu; somewhere I am actually living this other life. There are places where the world is stretched bubble-fine and I can glimpse those other existences, just for a moment.

'I realise you're feeling adrift at the moment,' my sister calls after me, trying to colour her voice with sympathy rather than irritation. 'I know this has been a massive blow.'

If I lay down, howled, and drummed my heels in the sand, she could swoop to reassure me, but my stony-faced silence unnerves her. It's not been as much of an adjustment as she might think. I've grown accustomed to coping on my own. It was the nature of his job, the travelling, the absence. At first, he asked me to go with him and I wouldn't, annoyed he wanted me to play dutiful wifey at conferences and symposia. Then I became mired in the milky, sleep-deprived depths of the nappy ghetto and by the time the children were old enough to be left, guilt-free, with friends for a few days, he no longer asked.

It comes on to rain, and father stands outside, watching the clouds and willing them to pass. It's a guilty pleasure to sit indoors in the warmth, the radio playing old music, my sister curled up on the sofa with a book. The children have found an ancient jigsaw puzzle, and seize on this steam-age novelty with wonder. My youngest gathers pieces into one sticky paw and clutches them tightly to stop the others placing them; they laugh as they hunt for straight edges with an avidity that surprises me. There's a sensation of fullness in my chest, and I let it rise, test the warmth of it and find it good. I can't speak, don't move, because happiness is evanescent, and if I try to hold on, it will burst. But the moment stretches out. This is contentment, I realise; less wild than happiness, but better, somehow sweeter.

My father returns with a slam of the door and a rush of cold air. 'It's almost time,' he says, portentous with excitement. 'You boys will stay up late tonight, and when it's full dark, we'll watch the Northern Lights. The colours will blaze across the sky like the most incredible fireworks you've ever seen...' He sighs with happiness.

'But why?' My middle boy demands, always needing his facts pinned down.

'We're being bombarded with particles shot from the sun; the colours they make depend on their altitude and which gases they react with,' Dad says.

'Awesome,' says number one son, ever-polite, but my youngest looks anxious, his nose wrinkling as a thousand questions bubble to his lips.

'Finnish people say the lights are made by an Arctic fox flicking snow crystals into the air with its tail,' I quickly tell him. 'And people up here call them Merry Dancers, say they bring luck to anyone who sees them.'

Dad smiles, gratified that I've researched his favourite

phenomenon; my sister looks at me over her book with speculative eyes. I don't tell them the other stories I've found and treasured; that the lights make a rift in the sky, a liminal place where reality breaks down.

I bundle the children into scarves and hats, the smallest so layered with warmth he can hardly walk. We climb the dark rise of the dunes, blackly humpbacked against the night sky, then look out across the sea. My father glances over towards the west, and I see his mouth open soundlessly, his face suddenly aglow. A sweep of colour curves across the heavens, a sky-wide display; swooping, rippling, ever-moving. There are tumbling sheets of poison green and luminous violet and electric blue, tinged at their liquid edges with amber and scarlet. They are triumphant banners of translucent silk, the swirling skirts of dancing goddesses, the campfire reflections on Valkyrie breastplates. I sense a fizz and crackle in the icy air, wait for thunderous rumbles or the cries of far-off battle, but no; it is entirely, eerily silent. This is it; the threshold, the border between this world and the unknown.

'Do you see it?' My father demands gleefully, 'Do you see?'
My sister hugs the older boys closer, her face very young in the changeable light. I lift my youngest and he curls around me, mittened thumb in his mouth, wide eyes uncomprehending but marvelling all the same, and I know he'll remember this the way I recall my harvest moon. The colours shimmer and fade before my eyes and I gasp, fearing that the vision is slipping away. I reach out my hand to touch the void.
I feel tears sheeting down my face and my father's hand on my shoulder.
'I'm feeling it,' I whisper. 'I'm actually feeling.'

I look around me, at the faces of my family; turned up to the skies and washed with pure dancing colour. I am here, where I should be, fully present in this version of now.

'We're here,' my father says quietly, 'We're always here.'

I know that's not true, not even possible; not with the way that my life tries to slide between the cracks, not with the unspoken threat of his bucket list lurking in the background. But for the moment, it's good enough.

Emma Seaman lives in Devon with her young family, and is a freelance Marketing & Social Media professional. She has been writing fiction for ten years, winning awards including the Jeremy Mogford Food & Drink writing prize and the Wells International Literary Festival Award. Her short stories have featured in eight anthologies published by Legend Press, Exeter University, The Yeovil Prize and The Harrow Press (USA). She finds inspiration in long walks on Dartmoor, lazy days at the beach, from the people she meets and the fascinating minutiae of everyday life. You can discover more about her writing at: www.emmaseaman.co.uk

EMILY DEVANE

Ruby Shoesmith, click, click, click

1. Ample

'Your first word is ample.' Mrs Barker paces between the desks. 'Ample,' she says again, stressing the 'p' sound so that her chest heaves forwards, unsettling the chain that carries her glasses.

Ample. I know this one. 'Am pull' – is that it? I tap my pencil against my chin and think of Judy Garland cradling Toto in her soft peachy arms. Something about the scene suggests *ample* – in the best possible way, of course. *The Wizard of Oz* is my favourite film. Mummy named me Ruby after Dorothy's slippers. She must have known. Best of all, my family name is *Shoe*smith. When people call out 'Ruby Shoesmith!' I click my heels in reply. *Click, click, click.* Then, ever so quietly, I whisper: 'There's no place like home', because I'd rather be there than here.

2. Puddle

'Number 2: puddle.' Mrs Barker rests her ample behind on

her desk. I scribble down the last word then have a thin
this one.

Puddle. I know a thing or two about puddles. On the
steps that led from our old flat to the bus stop, we used to ⌐
the tap dancing scene from *Singing in the Rain*.

'But Mummy, it's not raining!' I'd say.

'Imagine the rain, Rubes. Just imagine…' she'd say.

We began to take our umbrellas each time we went on the
bus, just so we could do that dance. Mummy's umbrella was
red with white spots and a twisty wooden handle. Mine was
black and yellow with eyes on the front and a smile, like a
happy bumble bee. One day it bucketed down with rain, just
like in the film, and Mummy cried – with excitement, I think,
but I can't quite remember. It's a long time since we last danced
on those steps.

While I'm thinking, there's a *tip, tap, tip, tap* on the skylight
above, and rain spots on the classroom windows. Through the
rain I hear Mummy's voice, clear as anything:

'Come on, Rubes. No-one's watching. Let's dance the light
fandango!' She twirls her spotty umbrella and dances the time-
step on the playground bench, grinning at me.

3. Bicycle

'3. Bicycle,' Mrs Barker says.

This is a hard one. Bicycle. *Bicycle*. I learned the letters but
they're doing a tap dance in my head and I wish they'd stay
still.

Since I turned eight, my bike's stayed in the shed. Mummy
sent the money for it when I was six, specifying that it must
be green, with an old-fashioned bell and those ribbons that
dangle from the handlebars. The first time I pedalled to the
park, Grandad held on to the back. Ross Hargreaves laughed
at the ribbons – he said they looked dumb – so I cut them off
with scissors.

'What did you do that for, Ruby?' Grandma asked.

ҭid they were dumb.'

ᵒn't let anyone call you dumb,' she

Grandad as he sipped his tea.

dly call me dumb when I'm not,' I said.

Mrs Barker calls out. I scribble down my answer

ᵪ was a German composer. Grandad plays his music
old record player in the dining room. The album cover
ossy. I picture it now: Handel's portrait; his name in swirly
nite letters. When Grandad plays that particular record he
pours himself a glass of something, his 'wee tipple', then sits
in his leather armchair, skinny ankles resting on the matching
footstool, and shuts his eyes. He knows every note.

'Put that in your pipe and smoke it!' he says. 'Beats *My Fair
Lady*, don't you think?' Grandad's eyebrows stick up in funny
directions.

Actually, very little beats Audrey Hepburn singing *'I could
have danced all night'*, but I keep that to myself. I know she's
miming but she does it so *beautifully,* and her nightdress seems
to glow, it's so white. When I kiss Grandad's whiskery chin
goodnight, he holds me close, his breath warm with that
night's tipple.

Handel, I write, humming and tapping my pencil against
my chin. But it's not Handel I'm humming, it's *'I could have
danced all night'*. And from her bench outside, wearing a
glowing white nightdress like Audrey's, Mummy sings, too.

5. Staring

'Number 5 - and this one's relevant to you.' Mrs Barker taps
Tamsin Mason on the shoulder. 'Staring. Like *Dolly Daydream*
here.' Tamsin's cheeks flush crimson.

Staring is something I do pretty well. It's one of my talents.
I can stare at the rain and imagine a whole memory playing in

my head like a film.

This time it's the car journey back from Wales, when visited Mummy. Thing is, I don't remember facts like da times but I never forget a feeling, or an expression on a pers face. The taste, something like sadness, on my tongue w Mummy said she was staying where she was in that whi white room surrounded by huge canvasses stained dark, th colour of scabs. And the sharp, chemical smell from the turps she used for cleaning her brushes. Grandma's pretend smile, and Mummy looking the other way so she wouldn't see it.

Later, I ate crisps in the car. I stared at the passing sky, thinking up names for the clouds: Jeffrey for the big, fluffy one, Claude for the long grey one, and Marcy for the rippled one that looked a bit like a sardine. Grandad put Handel on the tape player, while Grandma rested her bare arm on the window ledge and closed her eyes.

6. Inconvenient

'Number 6. Inconvenient.' Mrs Barker enunciates each sound.

Grandma taught me this one by breaking it down into smaller parts. 'Things are easier to digest when they're cut up small,' she said, writing down each part of the word.

'Like sausages?' I said, and she laughed.

It's good when Grandma laughs. Sometimes she looks at me and says 'Penny for them?' She wants me to tell her *what's going on inside that mind of mine.*

'Penny for yours, first,' I say, knowing she won't tell me. Perhaps she's worried about hurting my feelings. Being a mother to your granddaughter must be pretty in-con-ven-ient, I imagine. Just as she thought she'd hung up her mothering pinny, she's cutting up sausages again.

7. Ripple

'Number 7. Ripple.' Mrs Barker walks past my desk. She

r eyebrows, as if it's a regular part of

...es across the river. The memory
...ny mind like a fish coming up for a fly.
...miliar with. The man's face is shadowy.
...t faces but I can't quite remember his. I have
... m supposed to know him, that he's important.
...ng, confident, pulling back his shoulder before
...e stone from his hand with a flick of the wrist. We're
...g together and something about his smell – salty and
... – is comforting, and he's holding my wrist in his, and
...n jumping up and down with excitement at the stone, which
dances across the river almost to the other side, a line of ripples
getting smaller with each hop.

'Mama!' I'm saying. 'Look, Mama!' But when I turn to her,
the riverbank is empty, just like the bench in the playground.

8. Disconnect

'Number 8.' Mrs Barker says.

I haven't answered number 7. Was it stone? I can't remember
now. 'Mrs Barker,' I say, putting up my hand, 'what was...?'

'Later, Ruby,' she replies, pointing a finger in the air as if
she's putting me on pause. 'We'll go over any questions at the
end. Where were we? That's right, number 8. Disconnect.'

Disconnect. Grandma says this is like when you take the
lead out of the telly and put it into the video player. We must
be the only people who still have a video player. Grandad says
it works perfectly well. He doesn't trust digital stuff. It's all just
somewhere in the *ether*, he says: neither here, nor there.

Take photographs, one of his favourite examples. Grandad
reckons that people don't print them out anymore, they just
take more and more and more. More than they know what to
do with, he says. All stored somewhere up there in the *ether*
protected by a password that no-one can even remember.
Grandad keeps our family photographs in albums. He's very

particular about arranging them in the correct order, before pressing down the sticky pages ever-so-slowly, to avoid bubbles.

Sometimes, when I can't sleep because my head is busy, Grandad lets me drink milk. He has his 'wee nightcap' and we look at the albums together. The captions say things like: 'Scarborough, August 1987. Carol digging to Australia' and 'Heber Close, November 1985. Carol amid the roses.' In one, Grandma holds a baby to her chest. You wouldn't know from the baby's smiling, chubby face that it's Mummy. Grandma's hair was long and dark back then. She says the albums make her nostalgic, but Grandad and I like to feel nostalgic. It can be a good thing, once in a while.

'Do you think she misses us?' I sometimes ask.

'Your mother?' Grandad replies.

I nod.

'I'm sure she does, very much,' he says. 'She was just so young... and unwell...' He empties his glass.

Why does she not come back? I want to ask – but I don't.

I'm pretty certain it's got something to do with me. Why else would Grandad not look at me when he talks about her? I have a horrible feeling that it was me that made her sick. Because in every picture before she had me, she was smiling.

Disconnect. I write the word, thinking about how well it seems to fit. It feels as if Mummy and I have been unplugged from each other. Outside, the rain has stopped and the sky is brightening.

9. Wobble

'9. Wobble.'

I smile at this one. Each year I'm allowed to ask three friends over for tea and Grandma makes birthday jelly. She layers it like a traffic light – strawberry, lemon and lime – and serves it with ice-cream in paper bowls with a frill around the edge.

'Jelly on a plate, Jelly on a plate, Wibble-wobble, Wibble-wobble,

Jelly on a plate.' She sings as she dishes it out.

At my seventh birthday party, I lost a tooth. My gums were too numb for me to notice it at first. Then I felt it swilling around my mouth, along with the jelly and ice-cream, and I spat it out onto the table cloth.

'Tooth on a table, Tooth on a table,' Grandma began to sing.

My friends joined in: *'Wibble-wobble, Wibble-wobble, Tooth on a table.'* We all laughed and somehow it was okay that Mummy wasn't there. Grandma wrapped the tooth in a napkin for the tooth fairy.

'What a lucky day,' she said, when I hid it under my pillow that night.

10 Unlucky

'Last but not least, number 10: unlucky.' Mrs Barker leans against the bookcase. Her eyes skim our faces. I feel them rest on mine for a moment.

Un-luck-y. I can't remember which 'ck' sound to use. Grandma would know. She's good at lots of things, like making flowers out of tissue paper and knowing what type of bird is singing just by its voice.

Tomorrow is Mummy's birthday. This morning, before school, we made her card. I drew a lady with soft, peachy skin and a white nightdress, twirling a spotty umbrella in the rain.

'Let's make the picture happy.' Grandma said.

'Alright,' I said. 'But it is happy, if you think about it. Dancing in the rain is pretty fun.'

'How about some sunshine?' Grandma picked out a yellow crayon.

I drew a smiling sun and red dancing shoes on the lady's feet. 'Grandma, do we have glitter?' I asked. I made the red shoes shiny and put a rainbow in the sky.

'Perfect!' Grandma clapped her hands.

Words really aren't my talent, so Grandma helped me with

those. Ross Hargreaves says I'm dumb at them. What he doesn't realise is that the words are all there inside my head. All I need is more time to find them. It's a bit like when Grandad uses his record player and he has to take the record out of the sleeve and give it a dust before he puts it on the turntable. My mind gets a bit dusty sometimes. Or, it's as if there's a lead that's been disconnected. The one that goes between the word in my head and the pencil in my hand.

Mrs Barker starts collecting in the papers before I've had a chance to ask about number 7. I'm too busy looking at the playground bench when she comes to take mine. 'Ruby. Ruby Shoesmith!'

Beyond the bench, I see something, the beginnings of a rainbow – and beneath the table my heels go *click, click, click.*

Ruby Shoesmith J3

1. am-pull
2. puddel
3. ~~d~~bysicel
4. Handel
5. stering
6. in-con-ven-ient
7. ~~skim~~ man
8. dysconct
9. wobbul
10. un<u>lucky</u>

Born in Derbyshire, **Emily Devane** now lives and writes in London. She came to writing relatively recently when, having taken a career break from history teaching to bring up her young children, she embarked on a City Lit course – and was soon hooked. She recently won the Haringey Literature Live Open Studios Flash Fiction Competition and won second prize in the Flash500 competition. Her work has also been shortlisted for the Fish Flash Fiction and Flash500 competitions. Between short stories, Emily is working on a novel inspired by her fascination with Eastern European history. She tweets @ DevaneEmily.

ANNE CORLETT

The Witching Hour

I discover that we have a witch on the first night in the new house.

There's a faint scratching coming from outside the children's room, and when I open the curtains she's there, floating expressionlessly in front of the window, long, vague fingers probing at the glass.

When she sees me she turns and drifts away. But I've only just got downstairs when the scratching starts again.

In the morning I check the property information form. The sellers have ticked 'no' in answer to the 'any supernatural disturbances or paranormal activity?' question. I phone the solicitor, who sounds bored as he informs me that witches don't fall into the supernatural category. There's case law apparently.

I have more joy with the pest control man.

Witches can be tricky, apparently, but he's sure he can deal with the problem.

Mark walks past as I put the phone down. 'Who was that?'

'Pest control.'

'Expensive?' He leans across me to straighten his tie in the hallway mirror.

'Yes, but it needs sorting.'

'It's not that big a deal. There's other stuff that needs doing.'

'Of course it's a big deal. It's a bloody witch, Mark. Not a leaky gutter or some chipped paint.'

He shrugs. 'If you say so.'

'I do say so.' But he's already heading out the door.

That night, I hear that *scritch-scratch* once again.

The witch is glowing faintly in the moonlight, her skin almost luminescent. I realise that she has an odd, unsettling almost-beauty, that the night fits her, sleek and flesh-tight, as though she's been cut out of the darkness itself.

I jerk the curtains across, my heart thudding, dull and relentless against my ribs.

Out in the hallway there's faint shadow, up near the coving.

When I move closer I can see that it's damp, a chill discolouration with the paint just beginning to flake.

The pest control guy manages to sound simultaneously patronising and defensive. I bristle, silently.

'Yes, I know witches are tricky. They're pretty much renowned for it. If they weren't, I wouldn't need his astronomically expensive services, would I? I could just flap a tea towel and shout 'shoo!'

Still, good news. There's something new on the market. It's not cheap, but he's sure it'll do the trick.

'She's back.' I stalk into the living room and throw my phone onto the sofa.

'Is that mine?' Mark snatches it up.

'No, it's mine. Where's yours?'

'Who's back?'

'Who do you think?'

He shoots me a look of intense irritation. 'Are we playing twenty questions, or something? Who's back?'

'The witch.'

'Oh.' He picks up the remote. 'Well, she's not doing any actual harm. What's the problem?'

I don't have the energy to argue.

'Can you leave me some cash tomorrow?' I say, instead.

'What for?'

'To pay the pest-controller.'

'You pay for it,' he says. 'You're the one who wants it done.'

'It's a bloody witch. We can't just ignore her and hope she goes away.'

'I can,' he says. 'Look at me, ignoring her.'

He points the remote at the screen, banging at the volume button until the high-pitched commentary fills the room.

'What time are we due at your work thing tonight?'

He pauses in the act of knotting his tie.

'I thought you'd forgotten.' Then his fingers go to work again, twisting the maroon silk into a careful noose.

'Why didn't you remind me then?'

I didn't sleep too well last night. There was a faint, unidentifiable *creak, creak* coming from somewhere overhead, and my dreams were full of scratches and groans and great patches of ever-spreading damp.

'I thought you'd decided not to bother. What about the boys?'

'My sister's babysitting.'

'Oh great. The rabid feminist. We'll come back to find the kids wearing dungarees and comfortable shoes.' He picks up his briefcase. 'Better let her know about the witch. She'll want to invite her in for a spot of communing with the sacred feminine or whatever.'

Then he's gone, the slam of the door an echo of his contempt.

'You must be Kate.'

I turn to see a woman beaming at me.

'I'm Emily. Mark's told me so much about you.'

Really?

Emily has a hand-span waist, emphasised by a scarlet belt, cinched tight beneath a pair of impressively teetering breasts that jiggle gently as she quizzes me about myself. Faintly unnerved, I glance over to where Mark is holding court. He looks up, his eyes alighting on me, then flicking sideways to Emily. His expression changes. A swift spark of *something*.

That's when the first little bud of suspicion begins to swell.

He detaches himself, and heads over.

'Hi, Mark.' Emily's hand goes to her hair, tucking a stray strand behind her ear.

The bud ripens and bursts. My senses sharpen to forensic precision. I'm aware of every nuance passing between them, as though I'm suddenly pitch-perfect to meaning and undertone.

Emily seems determined to draw me into the conversation, as though she needs my unknowing complicity.

See? His wife and I are such friends.

Mark can barely look at me. I can feel his anger, simmering away. He's furious with me for being here to witness his betrayal. He's furious with me for being betrayed.

There's a heavy silence in the taxi on the way home.

I wouldn't have thought Emily was his type. I never found out what the last one looked like – only that she always muddled up 'lose' and 'loose' and didn't know how to use paragraphs. But I always thought he liked the pouty, dusky-haired type.

I contemplate asking him if he thinks I should go blonde, but I can feel that he's ripe for an explosion.

At home, my sister's lolling on the sofa, feet on the coffee table.

'Hi, Mark,' she beams.

He shoots her a look of intense dislike, and walks out of the room.

'What's bitten him?' She makes no attempt to lower her

voice, but I wait until he's out of earshot before replying.

'Little blonde thing called Emily.'

'Seriously? Again?' She lets her breath out in a huff of distaste. 'He's such an arse, Kate. Please tell me you're going to leave this time.'

'I don't know.'

'You mean no.'

I look away, feeling for a change of subject. 'Did you meet our witch?'

She nods. 'She was hanging about out there when I put the kids to bed. They don't seem bothered. Maybe if you just leave her alone, she'll take herself off eventually.'

'You sound like Mark,' I snap. 'I don't want to wait. I want her gone.'

I'm in no hurry to go to bed, knowing all that awaits me is the rigid disapproval of Mark's guilty back. After Liz leaves, I go to the bathroom and spin the taps. The pipes heave and a miserly trickle of discoloured water appears.

I swear quietly, and turn to the sink. The same grubby liquid dribbles out.

I stalk through to the children's room and yank open the curtains.

Sure enough, she's there again. I feel a bitter taste in the back of my mouth, as though her mere presence is enough to turn the air sickly and the water rancid.

In our room, Mark is propped up on his elbow. For a mad moment, I think he might be planning an apology. Possible responses hurtle and collide in my head as I undress and climb into bed. Mark's expression is unreadable as he reaches out and jerks back the covers. The chill night air pinches at my skin, and I shiver and reach for the duvet. He shoves it away and slings one hard leg over mine.

I meet his eyes. There's no connection there, no calculation.

This has nothing to do with any residual, limping passion for me, nor with any whiff of guilt. There's nothing in his eyes but a dull desire that has no reach beyond the confines of his own selfishness.

His hand is on my breast, his knee sliding in between my thighs.

I close my eyes, shutting myself into the darkness behind my eyelids, flailing for some distracting fantasy. For a moment my mind remains blank. Then, from nowhere, a thought breaks through.

I'm blonde-haired, shapely, the swell of my breasts balanced by the plump, tempting curve of my flanks. My red belt is a snare for unfettered groins. My lips gleam when I talk, the words mattering less than the shape my mouth makes.

Suddenly, he goes still, as though he can feel the press of those thoughts beneath my skin. Then he lets his breath out in a long, slow sigh that might almost be regret, if it wasn't for the way his hands tighten on my body.

'Say it.' His voice is rough-edged, urgent.

I open my eyes to find him staring at me, his expression dark with something that looks like hatred.

'Say it.' He leans into me, and I flinch.

Would Emily flinch from him?

Not a chance.

She'd smile, and stretch, and clench some secret muscles, tipping him into ecstasy with a practised twist of her hips.

Suddenly I understand.

'Say it.'

'I'm Emily,' I say, and then I lie back and think of nothing.

When he's done, I stare into the darkness. There's no point closing my eyes now. All my hidden places have been forced and emptied. Even my thoughts have been pillaged.

I recall the look of contempt upon Mark's face as he rolls away, and a long, slow shiver passes through my body.

'What are you doing?'

Mark's standing by the bedroom door, watching me as I drag at the resisting wardrobe.

'I can smell something,' I say. 'Like something's gone off.'

'You're imagining things.'

I pause for breath, shooting him a furtive look. I haven't been able to meet his eyes since the other night. I'm raw with tension, unable to keep still. There's a cold feeling in the pit of my lungs and a bitter taste in my mouth. The milk was off this morning. All three bottles. And I know who's to blame.

The pest-control man comes round later, burgeoning belly straining at the buttons of his shirt.

He brandishes a garish-coloured bottle at me.

'New product.'

I peer at the print.

Wiccaway.

He takes the lid off and a strong scent emerges. Lavender, and something unfamiliar.

'Rue. It's supposed to be the business.'

'It better be.'

He raises an eyebrow.

'There are things going on in the house,' I say.

'Things?'

'Leaks. A smell.'

He purses his lips. 'Could be related, I suppose.'

'Damp patches. And a noise, up in the roof.'

'It's an old house…'

'It's her.' I cut across him. 'I know it's her.'

The boys are fractious and unreasonable that evening. Bedtime is an extended battle, full of feints and forays and ill-tempered last stands, all fought to a soundtrack of high-pitched whining.

When sleep is finally secured, I collapse on the sofa with a glass of wine.

The smug *tick tick* of the clock slices at my seething thoughts until I look up and realise that it's nearly midnight.

The witching hour. That's what they call it.

Mark's still not home and I know, without any need to explore the idea, that he's tucked into Emily, snug and satisfied at his acquisition of a red-belted slut.

There's another damp patch, oozing, slow and insidious, across the ceiling, trailing a crack behind it. Upstairs, right at the edge of hearing, there's that *creak creak* that the pest control man couldn't locate.

I close my eyes and imagine myself somewhere else.

The clock ticks, a tap drips, the roof creaks and, low and insistent, and, beyond it all, there's the *scratch scratch* of the witch.

I imagine silence. A place with no clock. A place with no one to watch the clock for.

A place without *her*.

There's another sound, another click, and it takes me a moment to realise that it's come from inside of me. It's like the quiet snap of a tiny, unnoticed bone.

It's a breaking, a falling-away.

I rummage in the hall cupboard, searching among the detritus of our lives. A stray spider scuttles away, as I find what I'm looking for.

Upstairs, she's floating outside the kids' window as usual, her fingers scraping against the glass.

I stare at her for a moment, and then I reach out, turn the catch and open the window.

Just for a heartbeat, I think I see something moving behind her eyes.

I climb onto the window seat, kneeling up to look at her, and then I smile.

As she drifts towards me, arms outstretched, I look into her night-deep eyes, trying to read the shape of the shadows there.

And then I pull the axe out from behind my back, split her skull, and drag her downstairs to the Aga.

When Mark comes home in the early hours, he finds me

relaxed and replete on the sofa. The axe is tucked back in the cupboard and the Aga is burning low.

'Alright?' he says, with all the suspicion of a guilty man.

I smile at him.

'Everything's going to be fine,' I say.

Anne Corlett returned to writing three years ago after a thirteen-year stint as a criminal lawyer. She has completed two novels, for which she is represented by the Richford Becklow agency, and is currently editing her third. She also writes non-fiction for magazines. She has been placed, longlisted and shortlisted for various short story prizes, and won the local award in the 2014 Bath Short Story Award. She lives near Bath with her partner and two small children and is currently in the final semester of the Bath Spa MA in Creative Writing.

ANNA METCALFE

Sand

They abandoned the truck at the edge of the city and divided themselves between two jeeps. Seven men in the back of each, shoulders knocking, thighs pressed against thighs. The road soon lost its surface to potholes, boulders and the branches of fallen trees. The track they followed was dry and pale. It passed through villages and travellers' settlements, quilts of dust billowing upwards in their wake.

On the second day, the desert came into view. It was bleak: a thousand shades of ash. There was no space here for politics. Land stretched away, bare and open and lawless.

Days bled into one another. Had he been asked, he could not have said if it was Tuesday or Friday or Sunday, if it was August or September. The other men occasionally made mention of the date with regard to a birthday they had missed or the number of days since they had left, but he allowed this information to pass unacknowledged, forgetting it as soon as it reached his ears.

They drove with the windows down, dry air in their faces, sand running into sand in an endless incantation. Pitched against such a backdrop, he felt he was no more than an outline.

When night fell, it became cold. They wrapped themselves in coats and blankets and tied their scarves more tightly round their ears. Some days, they would stop at dusk and make a fire over which they could cook, where they would sit warming themselves, before they slipped back to the car, one by one, to sleep. At other times, they journeyed onwards in the dark, snacking on flatbread and rice brought from home, not knowing how much to eat, how much to save.

The driver checked the water every evening, counting the flasks doing sums on his fingers. He poured a little petrol into each of the containers so that the chemicals burned their throats as they swallowed but the water remained safe. Bitterness lingered in their stomachs as a dull ache. One or two of them had vomited when they drank too much. They learned. No one took more than their share.

One afternoon, in the full heat of the day, they saw another jeep a short distance from the track. Their driver pulled off the road and made towards it. They came to a stop.

'Fuel,' said the driver, getting out of the car. They followed close behind. The sand burnt their feet through the soles of their shoes, shifting beneath them and eluding their grip.

The windows of the abandoned jeep were open and it was thick with dust both inside and out. The keys had been left in the ignition. The driver opened the door, took it out of gear and tried to turn the engine. It whirred but did not start so the driver got out, flicked the latch on the bonnet and peered inside. A couple of others went to help him. The rest stood with their eyes closed against the sun.

He looked out over the dunes. There were dark shapes in the sand, a couple of hundred yards from where they stood. He walked closer, picked out the contours of limbs, the lines of a torso, a protruding hand or foot. He counted. Seven bodies – all men – and perhaps more beneath the surface. Six faces were veiled beneath headscarves. One was unmasked. A thin face, an aquiline nose, eyes wide open, whites yellowed. He called to the others. They uncovered the remaining six faces, regarding each one with care, fearing to see someone they once knew.

The driver gave instructions: take scarves and coats, check pockets for money. The spoils were gathered in a pile. There was a penknife, a few coins, a fistful of notes, crumpled letters. Photographs of wives and children.

'Should we bury them?' someone said.

'Don't waste your strength,' the driver replied.

That night, the wind was low. They slept on blankets spread across the sand. The vast and empty desert brought the moon and stars a little closer to earth. He poured his gaze into the darkness and was reminded of other skies from other times.

He dreamt of home.

He was standing in the doorway watching her sleep. Her body was covered by a single yellow sheet, which rose and fell with her breath. The rest of the room was still. No traffic, no breeze, no voices in the yard. He touched her cheek, her soft skin against his hand, but in the moment of his relief she disintegrated like ash in his palm, sand slipping through his fingers.

At the end of the next day, they reached a settlement. It was close to nightfall when the pale stone houses came into view. The driver said they could rest. It was safe. The streets were narrow, empty and silent as the sun got low in the sky.

From a passageway between two buildings, a tall man ran out in front of their car. The driver braked hard and they were flung forwards. They came to a halt at the man's feet. Then he passed them, running again, his arms swinging wildly at his sides. They watched the man through the rear windscreen. Every few seconds he turned his head to look over his shoulder. There were shouts, footsteps. Three more men emerged from the passage, in faded army uniforms, guns slung over their shoulders. Two of them went after the first man. One stayed behind, yelling something at their car in a language they did not understand. The uniformed man looked hard at the jeep and made to approach it, but the driver did not wait for him to reach them. They sped forwards, tyres screaming.

They took a sharp right turn into a lane that was only just wide enough for them to pass. His head hit the window, hard, and for a moment everything was dark. When his sight returned, he saw that they had looped back onto the road on which they had come.

The others were shouting, demanding to know what was going on. They received no response. The air in the car was still hot from the day and he could not speak. He held himself upright, perfectly still, and remained silent. A few yards from the edge of the settlement they were surrounded. Two trucks pulled in front of them, blocking their way, then two more trapped them in from behind. More men in uniform appeared, giving orders in the same unfamiliar language. This time the message was clear. Get out of the car. Keep your hands where we can see them. You're coming with us.

They were all handcuffed, except the driver, and divided between the four trucks. A few of them shouted and struggled but he was silent, head bowed, careful to avoid catching anyone's eye. During the journey that followed, every sound, every jolt of the truck made him start. He was surprised to find that the prospect of death frightened him after all.

They arrived at a prison where they were separated and placed in crowded cells. The smell was unbearable. People have died in here, he thought.

There were in excess of twenty prisoners in a cell of ten square feet; men, women and children, crouching on the earth, or standing with their backs against the walls. Heavy iron bars lay across the gate, which the guard closed behind him.

By this time it was well after dark, but no one in the cell

seemed to want to sleep. Mothers sat cradling children too tired to cry. Men stood. They were deathly thin, their skin grey.

Morning came. More guards went by. At around noon, they were taken from their cells and marched into an open yard. On all sides, uniformed men stood ready with guns. The prisoners were led to a counter where they each received a handful of cold rice before being escorted back and locked in.

An hour or so later, the driver came to see him.

'It's going to be OK. You can leave,' the driver said, 'if you pay, that's all they want.'

'How much?' he said.

'How much do you have?' said the driver.

He had enough. So did four of the others. They left with the driver on the morning of the third day. Three of their party remained. He had been right, he thought, not to know them, to forget their names.

The air in the jeep was stifling. He tensed at the slam of the doors. No one spoke. He was ashamed in ways he could not explain. Layers had been stripped away. The outside world seemed more luminous than before, the arched lines of the desert razor sharp. The sky was a deep, planetary blue; the sun a bright white disk. It emanated something more than light; a force unknowable and relentless. There were no allies. Even the land had turned against them.

He felt only exhaustion. No fear or hope remained. He would allow the days to pass one after the other. He would make no demands, ask no questions and he did not listen to the information the driver bestowed. As they drove, his eyes clung to rocks and high dunes, anything to break the horizon.

He didn't know how many days went by, each the same as the last, until, late one night, the edge of a city emerged. Tall buildings with lit windows towered before them in the dark. Smoke rose up from factories and into the sky. There were people on the streets wearing suits and smart dresses. He felt invisible, ghostlike.

The driver took them through the suburbs, skirting the city's checkpoints. They passed villages, farmland, industrial sites. They did not stop for the night. In the morning, as the earth tipped into light, the sea appeared on the horizon. He felt he could reach out and touch it, feel it flowing over his fingers. They arrived at the shore. He took off his shoes and bathed his feet in the surf. It was less than an hour before the boat would leave. He waited at a distance from the others. A man in a black shirt and trousers came to take his fare. He pulled crumpled notes from his pockets and sand fell from the creases, through his fingers, to the earth.

The boat was no more than a dinghy, turquoise blue, shallow and weak. They were crammed in well over capacity. If the sea were rough, half their cargo could be lost. He was jostled onto a bench.

They were lucky. It was calm, peaceful even. His tiredness endured, his head thrummed and his limbs were weak. He let his body sway and sink in time with the movement of the waves. It had been a long time since he had been at her side. She came to him now and he whispered her name under his breath, hearing nothing over the engine and the hiss of the sea. He put his fingers in his ears and tried again.

Anna Metcalfe was born in Holzwickede. She has lived and worked in Lausanne, Chongqing, Paris and Norwich, where she pursued her MA in Prose Fiction at the University of East Anglia. In 2014, she was shortlisted for the Sunday Times EFG Short Story Award. Her work has appeared in *The Best of British Short Stories*, *Lighthouse Journal*, *Tender and The Lonely Crowd*, among other places.

ALICE FALCONER

Cargo

When Rob gets home it is two in the morning. He takes the stairs to the fifth floor so the rumble of the lift through the thin walls of their flat doesn't wake Susan. He eases his key into the lock and, after the clunk of it turning, waits. The door creaks once then he is standing in the dark hall, soft clusters of coats brushing his face. Going into the bathroom he pulls the cord for the shaving light over the sink, rather than switch on the main light which starts the ventilation fan rattling. When he takes a piss he aims at the porcelain instead of the water.

As he cautiously turns the handle of the bedroom door and tries to edge it open, it gets stuck on a pile of laundry. He pushes a little harder till he can slide his body through the gap then picks his way between discarded clothes and stacks of DVDs, navigating by the chink of light between the blackout curtains. Sliding into bed, he waits for Susan's breathing to become slow and deep again, then pulls his duvet around himself. They have one each: hers thick, his lightweight. She is rolled up in hers. He moves toward her and presses his chest to her back through the padding, and she sighs and curls away from him.

When her alarm goes off he lies with his eyes shut, listening to her softly fumbling for clothes. She seems to pause by the bed, is she looking at him? Her fingers stir his hair for a moment and he nearly opens his eyes. Pretending to mutter something, he turns over. Just as he feels she is about to ruffle his hair again, he hears her leave the room.

The front door closes and locks. He falls back into sleep, waking again at ten am. He hasn't told her that he's adjusted his hours at the warehouse this week so he can start at eleven and leave as late as possible.

All day they've been pulling down film reels from the high metal shelving. Aluminium boxes the size of pizza cartons, dispatched two days before the Friday premieres. Rob completed an index card for each one, but the last went out half an hour ago and he has nothing left to do, could go home early, if he liked.

He left his phone here last night and has waited till now to turn it on.

Yesterday's message from Susan, *Back late again??* She cares, then. Still, he pushes the phone under a slipping stack of envelopes and green forms.

Into the player on his desk he slides a cassette he has taken from the News archives in aisle ten. He likes idling through old footage, finds it comforting. Everything has already happened. Volume off, he fast-forwards through a riot stopping at a panoramic shot of an island. Wide sandy beaches palm trees. The camera helicopters back to capture the whole atoll and the screen whites out in an explosion, followed by a perfect mushroom cloud rising above the islands.

'Oh, for God's sake,' he says, out loud. For a moment he'd thought it was Melanesia. Susan wanted to shoot her next documentary there, they would go if they got funding. They. Her and Miko. Mike Lenz who called himself Miko Lens.

When she told Rob about it last month he had just opened the fridge and was deciding what to add to the casserole.

'…cargo cults,' she said. 'Do you know?'

'Tell me.'

'The Americans used the islands as a base during the war, and they brought stuff the Melanesians had never seen. Guns, radios, cars. Planes full of canned food. Luxury everywhere. It changed things. Cargo, they called it. All this magical sudden wealth.'

'Amazing, sweetheart,' he said, responding more to the excitement in her voice than what she was saying. He took out the beef and set it on the counter, turned back to the fridge.

'After the war,' she said, 'the Americans took all the cargo and left. But the priests tell the people, don't worry. Just recreate what happened, that will call it back. So they go on parading with wooden guns, they carve headphones out of wood and sit in the old control towers, they wait.'

'Great idea for a film.'

'Why?'

'What?'

'Why's it a great idea?'

He stood there looking at three yoghurts on the top shelf, feeling aggrieved, picked on. They did this with each other – reassuring, praising. You didn't have to listen, exactly.

'So clever,' he said.

'Why?'

His mouth opened and he looked at the yoghurts. Raspberry, gooseberry.

'I suppose…' He tried to remember what she had just said. 'The cargo thing?'

He heard the door swish as she went out.

The TV is flickering: a suited man silently instructing a cluster of microphones. Rob elbows the box of index cards off his desk. It rattles against the metal strut of his stool then cards flutter across the floor. Even if someone saw, it's a strange enough gesture to look like an accident.

Buzz, buzz, like a bee crawling under the papers. His phone again. He ignores it.

To pick up and reorder every card will take perhaps three hours, which is just about perfect.

Later that evening, very late, he stops the front door just before the creak, dodges into the bathroom and flicks on the shaving light, though it makes him look so pale that he avoids his reflection, keeping his eyes down.

He considers making tea, but boiling the kettle would wake her. He pours himself a glass of water instead and takes it into the living room. The lid of the cedar jewellery casket he bought for her last birthday is open. He sits in the armchair, fiddles with the silver-framed photo of her, slightly out of focus, in a pink dress on a lawn. The edge of someone else's pink dress in the corner of the photo. His sister's wedding, March last year.

He smiles at the memory, gets up and goes to close the casket. It is as crammed with trinket boxes as ever. The first one he takes hold of flies up in his hand with its unexpected lightness. But he knows it contains the pearl studs she bought when they went to Kerala. And the long slim box will hold her grandmother's watch. And in the third will be the silver bracelet he gave her one Christmas.

The clock she had given him that same Christmas, the small rosewood carriage clock, begins to chime. He throws a dishcloth over it to mute the sound and leaves the room.

The bedroom is warm and dark when he eases the door open. He cannot make out the shapes of the tallboy or the wardrobe. The blackout curtains are tightly closed, he made sure of that before he left for work yesterday. He shuffles cautiously forward, feeling with one foot for obstacles. As he brushes against a pile of DVDs and feels it begin to shift, he bends and presses the stack upright again between his palms, then stands for a moment in the dark, his pulse rushing. Once in bed he lifts his head from the pillow so he can turn it over, and falls into a deep sleep.

When he arrives at work he sees his phone lying blank and dead on the desk; he left it here again last night. He prods it: nothing.

Today he will do a spot check of the film stock. He walks down the chill aisles, their air permeated with coldness from the metal stacks. Griff finds him around lunchtime.

'Coming to the pub tomorrow?'

'I'm making dinner for Susan, but thanks,' Rob says as he turns into the next aisle. He unrolls the master manifest again and continues to select films at random. Lazy stock checkers never check films above their eye-height, but he pulls at the rolling ladder and climbs up and down, filthy with scraps and rolls of dust, trying to concentrate. *Island of the Fishermen*, J22. *Magyar rapszodia*, R14. *Moscow Does Not Believe in Tears*, S19.

Last Sunday she had come home late. When he heard her drop her bag in the hallway he switched on the TV. She came in and sat in her chair and began to turn the empty water glass on the side table back and forth, her hand over the top of it. Or perhaps she did not even move the glass – just that he knew that nervous gesture so well he felt the tension in her hand, wanting to.

She said, 'We need to talk.' Then she laughed sourly at herself, at her own voice mouthing the cliché. She usually said anything deep or serious in an ironic tone, but there were some things on which irony had no effect. Like turning the glass and expecting it to look different. So that her bitter laugh did nothing to change those words: 'We need to talk, I have something to tell you.'

'Well, I have something to tell you,' he said.

She turned toward him, startled. 'You do?' A kind of relief in her tone.

'I've been looking up your project. Your cargo thing. Really interesting. I could help with some of that.'

She slumped back. 'I've finished the research now.'

He was holding onto the arms of the chair, looking straight ahead at the floor-to- ceiling window, the low evening sun dazzling in.

'It's called sympathetic magic.'

'Rob, please.'

'Life-size straw aeroplanes,' he said. 'Straw aerials.'

And the bulb had blown. It happened all the time, the wiring in the old building, chewed by rats and mice or just worn out, fizzing and failing, but it had a painful sense of drama now. The next act imminent. She cleared her throat.

He jumped up from the chair. 'I'll fix it.'

'Rob –'

'No, wait.'

'Miko –'

'Wait!'

As he hurried between the chairs he bumped into one, banging his hip, stumbled into the dark hallway, opened the hall cupboard. Something fell out, the drill probably, grazing his arm and clattering against the door.

'Are you alright?' she shouted

He said nothing.

'Are you alright?'

'Yeah.'

'Are you listening now?'

'No. Just let me fix the fuse.'

He felt for the plastic shutter covering the fuse-box, flipped it up and, running his fingertips along the switches, found the one that was down. Once he had re-set the switches he went into the study and turned on his laptop. He did not type, just waited till he heard her go into their bedroom, then another hour, until he knew she was asleep.

Un Asunto Privado is wrong. 1996. That shouldn't be there. He pulls the heavy box out from the shelves, spins it so it's flat against his body and tucks it under his arm. Climbs to the floor and makes a note in the manifest. It is one in the morning and there is nothing left to check.

It is raining again, and by the time he gets home his ears are numb and his trainers are wet through. He sits on the carpet to pull them off, to stop them thumping to the floor.

On the covered balcony he leans down to the herb garden she bought him for their anniversary. She had painted the planter Versailles green, changed her mind and painted over with Provence blue. After a winter of rain, green started to bloom through blue. But most of the herbs are still alive. The tight low cluster of rosemary, the single tall stem of basil. Coriander spilling over the edge of the pot. He could plan tomorrow's dinner. He twists off each fresh green leaf of coriander, leaving the pale yellow ones behind. He will make something simple, one of her favourites.

He gets ready in the bathroom, undressing under the weak grey light. He opens the bedroom door to the point just before it collides with the mound of laundry, and in thick darkness picks his way round the piles of clothes he knows to be there. In one practised movement he slides into bed without making the mattress sink too deeply, rolls his duvet around himself and curls onto his side, facing the curtains. As he falls asleep he hardly moves, making only a few slight adjustments to his position, keeping solicitously to his side of the empty bed.

Alice Falconer graduated from the University of East Anglia Creative Writing (Prose) MA in 2014. Before that she worked full time as a lawyer; she now freelances and writes in the gaps between projects. She is currently writing a novel. She tweets about books @alicefffalconer

ADAM KUCHARSKI

Mosquito Press

You know something's gone too far when you're sitting here flicking through a deck of cards, trying to decide which of the queens is prettiest. The phone rings again. It's probably Castle, drunk in one of the girlie bars without any pesos for a taxi. My eyes close, and the sound blends into the cocktail of car horns and air conditioning. I am still, my limbs weighing against the bamboo, waiting for that image to reappear in my mind. It never takes long. And there it is: a vast tapestry of agony stapled against my eyelids.

A chirp comes from above and I glance up at the gecko clinging to the plaster. It twitches, turning its head towards me, dead eyes staring down, then hurries across the ceiling into the shadows of the beams.

Today is my birthday. Sabina wanted us to go out for dinner, but only because she wants to go to that American place by the harbour, the one with the ribs and cheesecake and stars and stripes on the napkins. I said I was busy.

The lamp flickers. Or perhaps it's my eyes. I glance at my bedside clock, but the display is filled with meaningless red squares after yet another brownout. As I get up to collect my watch from the bathroom, I hear footsteps echoing in the corridor outside. The noise rises before stopping abruptly outside my door.

There is a pause then two slow knocks. I shuffle towards the entrance. Two more knocks. I twist the latch and pull the door open.

Per Müller is smiling.

'Night in?' he says. A bottle of San Miguel hangs loosely between his fingers, as if it belongs to someone else.

I shrug.

'Man, you gotta party on your birthday. You're thirty-five. We go out.'

I'm thirty-three, but Per wouldn't care. He produces another bottle and clutches my shoulder.

'Found a new bar in Malate, man. Very nice, yeah? Best in Manila.' He nods vigorously, as if trying to convince himself too.

I sigh. 'I'll get my wallet.'

'My car's downstairs. I meet you there.'

I turn off the air con and lift my wallet from the kitchen counter.

I think I'm thirty-three.

Downstairs, Per is sitting waiting in a grubby Mustang. As I climb in, he turns the key, producing a faint grumble. Three more tries, and three more groans. Finally, with a heavy press on the accelerator, the thing comes to life.

Per sighs. 'You live too far out. These roads are bad for my engine.'

Ten minutes later and we are on Epifanio de los Santos Avenue. The city's main artery is busier than usual, the flow of cars already congealing. Buses nestle closely either side, almost stroking our wing mirrors. Per ignores them, squinting at the road ahead.

The truck in front is stacked with crates, thick twine

holding them onto vehicle's rusty chassis, each box home to a squawking cockerel. There is probably a victorious fighter among them, the pride of its owner. The village next to mine holds cockfights every few weeks. I've only been once, dragged along by my Filipino neighbour. I couldn't see much of the main event for the crowds and the frantic betting. Replace the sandals and basketball jerseys with top hats and tails and it could have been Ascot.

The traffic eases as we pass the city centre. We drive north, away from the familiar tower blocks. After a few minutes, Per taps on the fuel gauge. The needle has been resting against the red line since he left his apartment. As we reach the seafront, we swing into a petrol station. A boy extinguishes his cigarette and runs over.

'Full, sir?' he asks as Per rolls down the window.

Per nods. The uneven hum of the pump begins, and I close my eyes while we wait. When I open them, the boy is standing next to Per's window, grinning. Per passes him a pair of tattered banknotes. The boy welcomes them into his cupped hands then stuffs the cash into his money belt.

I spot the American place as we turn onto Roxas Boulevard. Ahead, a Jeepney swerves to avoid a child selling those miniature calamansi limes, its jeep skeleton dressed up in mirrored metal like a flamboyant Frankenstein.

'You hear about the accident?' Per says as we pass the new film centre.

'Apparently the scaffolding collapsed?'

'Yeah, but you know what happened later?'

I mumble something about a public statement.

He glances in my direction. 'Before that. I heard they were behind schedule. Workmen fell into the cement, so they seal in the bodies and carry on. Fucking creepy.' His fingers stretch out over the steering wheel. 'Still, what a story. Wish I take a picture.'

Per is a journalist with a weak grasp of tenses and morals.

I'd known his editor in Bangkok, back when I was an embassy liaison. I met Per in '75, in a poor excuse of a bar that was my local at the time. That was the year I…

The car comes to a halt.

'We're here,' Per says.

I open the door and thick warm air pours into my lungs. We're in a side street. There are no road markings. Trickles of water flow over the unfinished tarmac. I can feel the image appearing again. I see the pain, the piercing eyes, hands clutching, hoping.

A car horn sounds in the distance. An ageing van rumbles through a red light, continuing down the road into Malate. The street is lined with bars. Girls linger outside, cropped dresses clinging to their flesh, smiles appearing and vanishing as quickly as a wallet could open and close. As we walk along the road, a girl with waist-length hair threads her arm through mine.

'Join us for a drink?' she says, placing a hand on my chest, her silver bikini pressed against my side. I decline, and we wander on as they mutter insults.

Ahead, a trio of businessmen stumble out of one of the bars, grinning.

Per points to the entrance. 'That's it.'

The hostess winks at me as we walk through the doors. We descend stairs covered with tattered carpet and enter a sprawling room, hazy with smoke. Quilted black walls surround us, bordered by stained velvet curtains in a deep red. Is this what the waiting room looks like in hell?

I feel a hand stroke my back and turn round to find a girl staring back at me with a bright, insincere smile. Her dress hangs loosely on her small frame. God knows how old she is.

She flicks her hair back. 'You want a drink with me? I like cocktails. Martinis, like the Bond girls. Do you like the Bond girls?'

I shake my head. 'No thanks.'

'Come on, you don't have to be shy.' She raises her voice as she says "shy".

Per and I move towards the bar and she follows. I shake my head again. 'Sorry. Later, perhaps.' I take a seat on one of the faux-leather stools and pick up a menu. The girl sneers at me and struts away towards a man sitting alone in the corner on a chaise longue.

Per has already ordered. I nod and smile at the cues. I am drifting, sleepwalking. There are silhouettes behind the flimsy curtains, shadows that are nothing and everything. Lamps burn beside the shapes. There is incense in the air, tangling with the smoke, clinging to my nostrils.

A drink appears in front of me. The liquid is a dull blend of orange and yellow, like the embers of a neglected fire. With a slice of pineapple on top.

'It's his birthday,' Per tells the barmaid, passing her a handful of pesos.

'How old are you?' she asks, leaning towards me.

On the other side of the room, the man on the chaise longue is stroking the girl's hair.

'He's thirty-five,' Per says.

Perhaps I am.

Per examines his piece of pineapple then drops it back in the glass. 'You know I see Castle yesterday?'

'Did he tell you about this place?'

Per laughs. 'No, I tell him about it. He's busy with writing now.'

'Last time I met him he said he was planning something about our friend Marcos.'

'Article for your *Telegraph*?'

'Don't think he's done anything for them since Vietnam. His last few pieces have been in American papers. I guess the old man was getting homesick.'

'Maybe. Anyway, he brought that girl of his.'

'Maria?'

'Nice girl. Small ears.' Per has a thing about ears. 'She said they took her aunt.'

'They?'

'The government guys. She was working for one of those underground newspapers.'

'Mosquito Press?'

Per pretends to swot away an insect. 'Yeah, her paper loves stinging Mr President.'

'So what happened?'

'The guys come in the night. Tuesday about 3 o'clock. The aunt was sleeping.'

'Where did they take her?'

'Dunno. Some warehouse. She thinks it was east somewhere.'

'Then what happened?'

Per takes a gulp of his cocktail. 'When they arrive, they pull her into the room and undress her. Then… then they tie her against a block of ice. Huge block, like a bed. They leave her there until she begins to freeze.'

'Christ.'

Per finishes the last of his drink. 'He didn't help.'

The barmaid picks up the empty glass and places a fresh napkin by Per's elbow. 'Same again, sir?' she asks.

Per nods.

I watch the man on the chaise longue leave with the girl. He'll probably take her home and conclude their arrangement. In a bar like this, everything is an arrangement. No price brackets, no back rooms. No time limits. You can find those places, of course, if that's your thing. Grubby rabbit warrens filled with stained sheets and broken consciences. Handfuls of pesos exchanged like it was a gas station. But no money will change hands here. Not directly, at least. It's just overpriced cocktails and "service charges". It's all a game. An arrangement.

I turn back to the bar. Another drink has appeared beside me. Per is lighting a cigarette, one of the bootleg American packs. His expression brightens. 'I tell you I got a call from

Rogers earlier? He likes my pictures, talks about exhibition in New York.'

'Which ones?'

'Most from Thailand in '77. Plus a couple from the year before.'

'Cambodia?'

Per shakes his head. 'No not Cambodia.'

'Do you ever think about that night in Phnom Penh?'

He pauses. 'The one with Castle and the Vietnamese wine? Ha! That was crazy.'

'You know the one I mean.'

Per pulls the cigarette from his mouth, smoke seeping from between his lips. 'I forget. You need to forget.'

'We should have helped them.'

'We would be killed.'

'You know they were unarmed?'

'So were we. I was shooting camera, not Kalashnikov.'

'Remember that group behind the church?'

Per taps his cigarette against the ashtray. 'Have a drink. Stop thinking. Where's your girl, Sabina? You should go see her.'

'And what? Sit in a restaurant and eat steak and talk about films?'

'You need a whiskey.'

'We let them go ahead with it just so we could get a story.'

'I'll get you a whiskey.'

'So you could get another photo.'

'Which one you want? Scotch?'

'I can't remember the last time I slept properly.'

'Nobody can sleep. Too many fucking mosquitoes.'

'Do you care?'

'Does anybody care? All they want is beer and girls. And money.'

I watch the ice melting in my glass. 'Yet we just end up alone, don't we? We just sit there, flicking through a pack of playing cards, wondering who looks prettiest. You know that, right?'

Per stubs out his cigarette and smiles. 'It's the Queen of Diamonds. Everyone knows that.'

Adam Kucharski is a lecturer in infectious disease epidemiology and an award-winning science writer. Born in Bath, he studied at the University of Warwick before completing a PhD at the University of Cambridge. He was the winner of the 2012 Wellcome Trust Science Writing Prize and his articles have appeared in the Observer, Scientific American and BBC Focus. His book *The Perfect Bet* about the relationship between science and gambling will be published by Profile Books in spring 2016. He currently lives in London.

FRAN LANDSMAN

Big and Brie

My name is Big – but I'm not. I'm small. They call me that because my surname is Spender – like 'Big Spender' – which is a song. But I'm not a big spender either. In fact I've only got £9.17 to last me till next Tuesday.

Something big is going to happen to me though. Actually it's big for me, but even bigger for Brie. She's my girlfriend and she's the one having a baby. It isn't my baby, but that doesn't matter. I'm going to be its dad, and I'm going to love it with all my heart. I'm going to make up for all the children we've had taken away from us.

Me and Brie. Brie and Me.

My real name is Keith Spender. I'm thirty-two and I'm not stupid. Brie is Brie Rose. She's thirty-four and she's not stupid either. Neither of us is stupid – we're just not clever. Can you understand that? Well, if you can I'd be surprised because no one else ever has.

'Probably because they're all stupid,' Brie said once.

We've both always been told that we couldn't do anything right, and people have always laughed at us and called us names which I won't repeat. I'm a nice person. I'm five foot two inches tall, my hair is a bit sticky-outy because Brie cuts it, and my lucky T- shirt says 'FINGER LICKIN' GOOD' on the front. I'm good at finding my way to places and I can read and write. Brie is taller than me and she's gorgeous. Huge and gorgeous. She doesn't wear a bra and she can do tapestry. She's really good with numbers and she looks after all our money, what there is of it. She pays the bills, gives me spends for my fags and bus fares, and sometimes she can do nearly all a sudoku.

We met at college a few months ago when we were both sent on a cooking course. I fried the potato and Brie boiled the baked beans. That was our first meal together and I couldn't take my eyes of Brie's ginormous boobs. She had a ginormous arse too, but she was sat on that so I couldn't see it then. I had to tell her how I felt, even though I'm a bit shy. It went like this: 'You're gorgeous.'

'I know.'

'Do you want to go out with me?'

'Not really.'

'Oh, go on.'

'All right.'

Everyone in the class cheered, and that was it. Me-Brie. Brie-Me.

I was living in a poxy caravan at the time, so I moved into Brie's flat a few weeks later. Brie'n me didn't have secrets and she told me straight away that she was going to have a baby in six months. I promised I'd be its dad and Big doesn't break promises.

I'd always cocked things up before, but now I'd met Brie it was going to be great. I was going to look after her and make everything nice.

Last weekend I painted our bedroom glossy green like a garden because it was going to be the baby's room too. It was a bit bright, but I found three tins of Dulux gloss in "Lime Sublime" in a skip. When it dries I'm going to paint some rabbits round the bottom, and Brie is making a tapestry for the wall. When the Jeremy Kyle and the soaps have finished on the telly, I paint and Brie fills in bits of the ducks on her tapestry with blue silk.

'Ducks are yellow,' our social worker said on the Monday. She was Brie's social worker really, but now that we were together she was ours. I liked that we even shared a social worker, so we could not like her together. We hated bloody Jane. She's only supposed to come round to make sure we don't need anything, but she thinks she's got the right to criticize. Anyone would think she was Jeremy frigging Kyle in drag.

'Well, they're not yellow in this house,' I told her, but it was too late. Brie had already burst into tears.

When she cried I didn't know what to do. Everything I said made it worse. Even school wouldn't have taught me how to deal with a crying Brie. In the end I made her a cup of tea and stroked her hair. That seemed to do the trick.

We were both sad about our children who'd been taken away. One of Brie's and two of mine. We really were. But there's a 'system'. That's what Jane said. 'There's a system and it's for the best.' It wasn't bollicking best for me and Brie though.

I know Jane thought I didn't care, but I wasn't going to tell her how I felt. I didn't even like her – the stuck up cow. There she went – Mrs. No-Arse. Mrs. No-Tits. I hated the way she let herself into our flat just because the bell didn't work and we never heard her knock. We did hear, actually – we just didn't answer.

She'd creep in wearing those colossal rubber clown clogs that never made a sound. Not like Brie. She wore proper ladies' shoes and she never snuck up on me. In fact her shoes made a racket because she squashed the back bits down with her feet. You could hear her coming for miles.

'I was a career girl,' Jane said, like it was something to be proud of. You don't need a certificate to know that's arse about tit. They could have put her kids in care and she wouldn't have noticed. Too busy sticking her nose in where it wasn't wanted.

We tried asking her questions but she never answered. All we knew was that she had a dishwasher, a deep fryer and no telly. 'Oh, my life's quite dull,' she'd say. We didn't doubt that, what with no telly.

On Tuesday she came round when Brie was out shopping. She let herself in as usual.

'Hello. Hello – anyone in?'

'No,' I said.

'I'm glad I've caught you, Keith.'

Then she sat herself down on the sofa.

'I wouldn't sit there,' I said. 'I just spilt some ketchup.' That made her jump all right. Brie would have laughed. 'D'you want something to wipe your trousers with?' She nodded and I got her the dishcloth, which she held between two fingernails as if it was something I'd sneezed. It was a bit manky I admit, but not as manky as her arse.

Eventually she sat herself down on the pouf and said, 'I want to talk to you about the baby. Have you thought about it? Properly thought about it?'

What I thought was that this woman could take our baby away, and I had to say the right thing.

'It wouldn't be loved if it grew up in care,' I said, and that seemed to be the right thing because she looked at me then.

'That's true. Love *is* important to a child, but it's not everything.'

'We can learn the rest.'

I believe you can,' she said, 'but you're going to have to let us help you. You tell Brie that. We don't want to take her baby away, but you've both got to prove you're willing to learn. We'll be keeping a close eye on you.'

'Who's we?' I wanted to know. 'Social workers, family project workers, home support worker, health visitor. Is Jeremy Kyle coming too?'

She ignored me, but then what does she know without a

telly? Instead she asked to see the nursery. I was proud of my paint job till she pointed out that the tins looked old and the paint might have lead in it.

'You can't take a risk with lead,' she said.

Do babies lick walls? I doubt it.

'OK,' I said. Mustn't upset Mrs La-Di-Da-Paint-Expert. That *would* be stupid. When Brie got home later I didn't mention the paint, but I did tell her that they were going to let us keep our baby, just so long as we let them help us.

'I don't want them round here all the time. Why won't they leave us alone?' Brie said before she burst into tears again. That made me cry. That made Brie cry even more.

I tried tea and it didn't work, but Brie stopped when I said crying might upset the baby. 'I don't want to make the baby sad,' she said, and I told her she was going to be the best mum in the world. I gave her another kiss and pinched her big fat arse. Then she hit me and I fell off the sofa and spilt my Coca Cola. That's what happens all the time in our house.

It was really hot on Thursday when Jane came to take Brie to hospital for a scan. She'd been puking bucket loads so Jane offered her a lift in her yellow Ford Fiesta. Custard-on-wheels, Brie called it. We'd rather have gone together, but it took two buses each way and would have cost a few quid in bus fares.

'If you let Jane take you we can spend the money on some popcorn chicken for later.'

'Popcorn Chicken? Well, maybe. Okay.'

I set to work painting the rabbits brown. I knew the colour of rabbits and I wasn't going to have Jane telling us we'd got something else wrong. Four hours later the first one was the size of a small horse, and Brie still wasn't home. My phone didn't have any credit so I just watched TV and waited. Eventually I went and got the popcorn chicken. I ate mine and put Brie's in the oven to keep warm.

Six o'clock and I heard the front door open. I thought it was going to be Brie, but it wasn't. It was Jane in her stupid pink rubber clogs, creeping in again as if she owned the place.

'Where's Brie.' Jane just stood there for a minute. 'Where is she?'

'They're keeping her in. The baby's heartbeat is very faint.'

She patted my arm, but I wanted a soft warm hug. A Brie hug. It was probably for the best that Jane didn't try because a social worker hug would have felt more like a cuddle with a lamppost.

'Get some things for her and I'll take you to the hospital.'

I was so scared I was shaking, but I got a plastic bag and filled it with stuff I thought Brie would like. A can of Coke, a Kit-Kat, the popcorn chicken, nightie, my toothbrush because it was newer than hers.

When we walked into the ward I could see Brie sat up in bed. She was attached to machines and her eyes were red.

'I've been crying,' she said. 'But I'm better now. The doctor says the baby's okay. Only one sleep and I can go home. I'm hungry.'

She ate the popcorn chicken, then we kissed and kissed. After a while Jane started coughing then she took me home.

When I got in I Shake-and-Vac'ed the carpet so it would be all nice for Brie. I used a whole tub. Then I took the sheets to the launderette and sat there till midnight so they were really dry. As I walked home I looked out over the city lights. All those clever people in those houses, and I knew we'd be as good a mum and dad as any of them.

Jane brought Brie home the next afternoon and didn't even come in the house. That was a surprise. I'd expected her to be marching in and telling me what to do. Make sure she rests. Make sure she puts her feet up. Make sure she eats properly. I knew all that, and I was glad I could do it without being told to. It made it nicer

Brie was really pleased with the clean sheets, but we had a row about the Shake- and-Vac because she said it stunk worse than the hospital. It was better after I'd opened the windows and sprayed deodorant around. We had chips for tea, and we shared a can of Coke.

Then Brie said she'd made a big decision when she was in hospital. 'Jane wants us to let all those buggers help us, and I've changed my mind.'

'What if the buggers tell us we've got to Shake-and-Vac?'

I'll tell them to piss off,' she said. Then she pushed me off the sofa and spilt the Coca Cola. I said that happens all the time in our house, didn't I?

On the Saturday I took Brie to the park to look at the ducks so she could decide what colour they ought to be. We didn't see one yellow one. Not one.

'You'n me are right about some things,' I said to Brie.

Fran Landsman is a documentary filmmaker and writer and lives in Bath. Her films include the Bafta nominated *My Family and Autism, The Secret Life of The Classroom*, which was filmed in Bath, and *Save The Last Dance For Me* for the BBC Imagine Arts Strand. Fran's short stories have been successful in the Bridport Award and the Bristol Short Story Award, and have been broadcast on Radio 4. They form part of a fractured novel called *Rocket Surgery*. She also has poems published in three anthologies.

FIONA MITCHELL

The Quiet Numb of Nothing

The Woman in the Yellow Headscarf takes the berry-full basket from me. Her mouth opens and closes, but my ears swell with nothing. I turn away from her, so she won't see the bad in me. It leaves me alone in the scrub; it shuts me in huts.

I steal a look then. She has a lump of baby on her hip and her mouth lifts at the sides. I search for sharp teeth, but the eyes on her are full of shine. There's no pelt on her, no whiskers, no sand-coloured fur. She doesn't shake her head the way Father does.

At any second, the other pickers, blue and green stoops in the field, will realise that I'm a girl without sound. Kob Girl, that's what they'll say. Like them boys with dirt under their fingernail claws, with fast legs and hard arms. Though I'm quiet as an antelope, there is a roar inside of me.

Headscarf Woman gives me another basket. I carry on picking. The colour and gloss on the berries lifts me off the ground some. I squat and pick, pinch and pull, and start to fill the basket with bright little dots. The Woman's lips go wide, but I don't speak back.

My first day will be my last when she realises the badness I bring, and I'll go back to the hut making smoke on the way with my toes.

I didn't always have ears full of nothing. Flowing water goes Sssssh. Coughing makes an Uh-uh-uh. I lost them sounds when the sweats thrashed me, made their home inside me.

After that, when I spoke, Father's eyes narrowed like I was making the worst kind of noise.

I've tested everything with my mouth since. That boy's fingers were watery despite the dirt and splats of paint. He wiped them on his trousers. I put a stone between my teeth later, and it felt dangerous. A big thing like that could close a throat, I thought.

I'd become a Bad Omen Kid, a Kob Girl, so I sat inside the hut where no one had to look at me. It was only when I was inside that the lines left Father's face.

Even my little brother, Alanyo, slept as far away from me as possible. Then the Woman, her hair wrapped in stripes, turned up and talked with Father who shook his head a lot.

I risk a look at her now, the puffed sleeves of her yellow Gomesi. She's not picking; she just stares at me, letting my badness settle on her like sweat. I know then that I'll be home by noon where the clay under my feet will stick me to each slow moment.

She looks away. I pull another red berry from its stalk, put it into my mouth and chew. It burns my tongue, not no spark, nor smoke. I am fire full, stinging. I suck in air, but it only makes my mouth hotter.

I run to the pipe, dunk it down and drink, but it does not make a dent. I dance, feet stamping the dust and Scarf Woman, she shakes her head. I'll be home for sure now, with a mouth in flame. I flap my hands.

Scarf Woman gives me a beaker of milk and I drink it down. The heat in my mouth disappears. The Woman points at the kicked-over basket and arches an eyebrow. But she does not tell me to leave.

It has been a shorter day than most, but still there is the long walk home, through greedy branches and messy reeds. The soles of my feet knead stones.

A Kob runs across the clearing and fixes me with its stare. Its coat is the colour of nut; its horns are striped. That antelope wouldn't last a finger flick if she had no ears like me.

The coins are cold in my pocket, the sun warm on my face. There is a breeze and then bam goes my back. The pain is the colour of them berry bells, the colour of the hay between my legs each month, though that hasn't happened in a while. I flip round and there are four of them, the boys, mouths snapping, cheeks pink with glee.

One of them raises the jagged thorns of the stick. I shape my mouth around a No, but whatever comes out, it makes the boys laugh harder, pinker. And the stick comes down again, bloodying my nose. The biggest one, the one with the dirt nails and the spots swollen with pus, puts his fingers up to his head and makes Kob horns with them. Kob. His quiet teeth bite the air with the word.

My thin, deer legs topple me then. My tongue finds the space where he put my tooth out that first time when he unzipped his trousers and scooped out that turkey neck of skin. It's only when I look at him now, the fingers still horns on his head, the mouth still laughing, that I know he's the one that put the roar inside me, even though all three of them had a go. He is older and bigger, his hair longer than the rest. He has the whiskers of a lion and a threat in the eyes.

I curl myself up and press my hand to my stomach where the thing hoofs through my inside water. It sends the taste of metal into my mouth. I rub at the stretch of scar in front of my left ear where Lion Boy hunted me the last time.

Kob, he calls me again, his mouth shaping the silence. The dress on me makes a breeze as Lion Boy smacks the stick to my ankle.

I try to loosen myself, so it won't hurt like before. He holds me down with a foot, his shadow blocking the heat, and the moment is a slow sinking marsh with panic in it. Something unexpected happens then. The sun comes out. I have to shield my eyes from it.

The neighbourhood boys are running away, dints in the dirt from their feet. The thorny stick lies across the clearing like a piece of broken train track. Then there is the silver taste of fright as something shakes my shoulder. I stiffen my fingers into a gun, so I might stun whatever it is that's about to rip through me.

The Woman with the Yellow Headscarf stands there. The baby is fixed now to her front. She is frowning a river gorge into her forehead, her mouth slicing up words I don't hear. I shake my head, look away, try to move my shoulder from her shudder touch, but she won't let go.

She bunches my T-shirt in her fist and pulls me up. She is orange cross, her mouth moving fast. I look to the baby, the froth of hair on the back of its head. All that snapping hasn't woken it.

The Headscarf Woman covers her ears with her hands. She bends and goes face level with me, opens her mouth wide and whatever she says, it isn't *Kob*. I concentrate, but no amount of wishing can make me read lips. My frantic head settles into the quiet numb of nothing again. The quiet numb that no mouth dancing, no hand swaying can break through.

Her forehead crease is a canyon now. She smacks my hand and when I look down, I see that she has put a coin there, a coin that must have fallen from my pocket. She tramps away through the dust.

I walk on, eager to be back at the village before anyone else comes through the bush. The pitch has swallowed all the yellow light by the time I turn into the smallholding. I go towards the mud hut, put my hand against the wall bearded with grass.

Alanyo is asleep on the mat. I don't look at Father, who is wafting a peacock feather to and fro in front of the boy's face. I scoop up the leftover matooka and wipe it lardy onto my tongue. It is the hug of my gone Mama, the kiss of my working-away sister. I curl myself into a ball, beige with an almost full stomach and the aching limbs of walking.

In the morning, I pat down my pockets, but the coins are gone. Father nods and I turn away. Alanyo picks up his schoolbag, his hand dimpled around the frayed handle. Father bends and kisses him right there between the eyes, and Alanyo goes away on ten to two feet, a shadow over him fat with the words and numbers and pictures and sounds of his school day.

I start to walk, head twisting backwards every ten steps to make sure there is no one behind me in the scrub. The grass blades my feet. I run, my arms stretched out in front of me as if feeling the way. I stop then and what is it that makes me suss movement - a change in my inside temperature, some emotion that makes the sides of my eyes turn grey? I shimmy down the hillside and hold tight to a twisting vine. Lion Boy thrashes his way through the straying branches, over the felled logs, his feet making the gravel roll. I keep my eyes on Lion Boy as he disappears and the grey in my eyes turns to chalk.

At the farm, I start my bending. And my picking. Three baskets full and I clock the flip-flopped toes of Headscarf Woman. She flips her head towards the barn with the rippled iron roof, her mouth a flat line.

It is too early for a break, but I follow her anyway. Perhaps she has brought in a witch doctor to make ugly faces at me, to push bottles of foul amber stench beneath my nose, to smack away my demons.

I follow Headscarf Woman into a room with pictures on the wall and people sitting. A tall, thin man in his twenties with an expressionless face on a blue plastic chair. An old lady with flabby, polished leather cheeks. A little boy with his chin in his hands, and a smile that says fun.

She stands at the front, Headscarf Woman, the baby strapped to her side. She tufts her fingers on top of her head. She points to a picture on the wall then stares at me. The other people make antlers with their fingers. The woman mouths a word that could be *Kob*. I look at the picture of the antelope on the wall and my cheeks redden; the roar in my belly shakes me.

I move towards the door, shoving the air backwards with my

fists. The grilled heat calls me outside, but one, two, three more pickers arrive. And then more pickers block the light in the doorway. I turn and Headscarf Woman is bouncing her hands in front of her. She points at either side of her mouth and pulls it back into a smile. She points to the lion drawing, claws her hand and pulls it backwards over her head. I think of Lion Boy with the spots and the trousers, the jarring and the taste of his salt dripping into me. I want to spit on the floor of this barn, this classroom, this whatever it is. I want to walk out. But the woman punches two fingers in front of her and points to a picture of a snake. A river of hands wave, point and pull.

I sink into the seat and conduct the air with my fingers. There is a pain in my belly, and the galloping and the teeth graze against the inner parts of me. The inside head butts, the jaw stretches wide. And I just sit there, fingers tapping and weaving.

Soon, I go to the front of the class and stand beside Headscarf Woman. I go up to the wall and point at the Kob. *Me?* I spell the word with my fingers. And she shakes her head. She spells letters slowly and the old lady sitting out there on one of the chairs smiles and nods. Headscarf Woman makes the word, *Joy*, her fingers cutting space, dividing it into parts until I hear the shape and the sound of the letters, the colour and taste of the word. The baby on her hip starts to squall, but I hear none of its cries. And the woman's hands go on moving. *My name is Pamela*, she spells. And the silent room is alive with noise.

We make a connection, me and Pamela. I stand there, my ears full of something that isn't sound. Her hands pluck at the air. And the thing inside me moves, not roaring now, just tilting ever so slightly. I do not turn away. My fingers twitch and start to slow dance. 'I am,' they say, weaving and turning. 'I am Joy.'

Fiona Mitchell is a features and fiction writer. This year she won the Frome Festival Short Story Competition and, for the second year in a row, her work has been shortlisted for the Bristol Short Story Prize. Her short stories have been published in the *Bristol Short Story Prize Anthology Volume 7 and 8*, the *Yeovil Prize Anthology* and various other places. She has just finished rewriting her first novel *The Maid's Room* and is editing her second novel, while working on ideas for a third. To find out more about Fiona's work, visit www.fionamitchell.wordpress. com and connect with her on Twitter @FionaMoMitchell

CHRIS EDWARDS-PRITCHARD

Ruby Slippers

The shoes were little red Nike Air trainers with eroded heels and laces that were fraying into spaghetti, and splinters of mud painted on to the breathable crosshatching. They were his wife's and now they were his. They belonged to him now, to Nathan. For a couple of months he had been their caretaker keeping watch over them until they could be worn again. Now he had full custody. After the first round of chemo he had placed them on the floor beside her bed, facing outwards, ready for her green-gown legs to swing out and her feet to nestle inside. Those were the days of acetaminophen and one or often two out of ten on the Pain Scale. Nathan would laugh with Lara about how the Pain Scale was a load of bollocks when neither she nor the nurses could fully quantify or understand ten out of ten. It was something to laugh about. Her whole face creased as she smiled, the way it can sometimes when you've been out in sun for too long. And that too was funny. Funny as in: how the hell are we going to cope with the destruction of your beautiful smile? Others became accustomed to the red Nike trainers. In particular her mother, Leanne, who would approach the bed with carrier bags of fruit and clothes and audiobooks, and say: hello Lara, and, hello shoes. As if the shoes were another of her children. Leanne would visit during the day with various friends and relatives, and Nathan would visit after work. They built a routine. They were on the same page for once. Leanne would even say the same things that Nathan would say: you'll be back in those shoes before you know it, more halves, maybe even a marathon, if your uncle Bill can run one so can you. And Lara would be like: yeah, I can do that. Somewhere in there, on a day when she was levelling at seven on the Pain Scale and the opioids were a low dosage she made Nathan enter her into the ballots for a few of next year's major marathons: London, Berlin, New York, Boston. The phrase Bucket List was used for the first time. Nathan asked her why she was talking about a fucking Bucket List all of a sudden and she told him not to swear in here, raising what was left of her eyebrows at the sleeping sweep of the ward. He grabbed the bed rail. But the lesions have shrunk, he said, and after the resection op you'll be clear, he said. Lara swallowed as if swallowing a small stone. She tilted her head. Would you get me a drink, she said, I've got a headache. Which was what she always said to diffuse arguments back home; arguments about doing the dishes and taking the dog out and leaving underwear in the bathroom and whose turn it was to be designated driver and whether they really had to go to Leanne's again for another awful Sunday roast. The night Lara had her colon removed both Nathan and Leanne sat beside her bed well past visiting hours and waited for her to wake up. She was in a side room now. 5b. A dusty lamp in the corner of the room was humming along with the heart rate monitor and the sat monitor and the SCD. The red trainers were waiting patiently by her bed. Nathan had placed them there. Why do you still do that? asked Leanne. She was knitting a small bobble hat for Lara's yet-to-be-born nephew whose estimated arrival was unfairly out of sync with his auntie's estimated departure. Nathan stood up and looked out of the window. It was raining. Leanne spoke again. Don't you think it's time we put the shoes away, she said, it's a constant reminder of everything she used to be and we don't think that's helping her. And continued knitting. Loop and thread and loop and thread. Nathan went to walk out of the room but right then there was a shuffle from the bed and a farting noise and then a faint murmur. Nathan rushed to Lara's side. Her eyes flickered open and then shut again. It's me, he said. It's me. Mouth open, lips shattered, shallow yellow tongue, drip taped to cheekbone, bones on show everywhere, elbows were the worst, only a suggestion of hair now, only a suggestion of human being. He wanted to tell her that it was their first wedding anniversary today and that he was sorry for not buying her a present. He'd been caught up with things. But the words didn't come out. Instead Leanne spoke. She said: you've got a nice new bag now my love. As if the ileostomy bag was a gift. Lara twitched her brow. Possibly a response, probably just a twitch. Nathan looked at his mother-in-law, like: that is the least funny thing you have ever said. The time for funny had long passed. A couple of weeks after that Nathan received a text message from Leanne which read: Lara a nine on Pain Scale now. He was just finishing up at work. He showed his boss Gary the text and all Gary could say was: fucking awful. Back at the hospital Nathan went to enter room 5b but found an old man in place of his wife. The old man said: not the face you're looking for son? And Nathan said: no but not far off. He went to the desk where a nurse was writing some notes on a whiteboard. Any idea where Lara is, he asked. 5e, she replied without even turning around. She pointed in the direction of 5e with her pen. Lara was asleep. She'd become real good at sleeping. Leanne was sitting by the window reading a magazine. Roy was also there. He had suddenly become a regular visitor. He was a Fulham fan, but the kind of Fulham fan that only went to games when they were facing relegation. She's on a high dosage of morphine, said

Leanne, it's really knocked her for six. The machines beeped and whirred and every now and then Lara's little feet would twitch and he wondered if she was dreaming about running. The shoes had gone. Where have the…? Where have the shoes gone? he asked. Leanne and Roy looked at him and looked at the floor and looked at each other and then looked back at him, towering above them, beginning to tremble. Her shoes, said Nathan, where are they? Leanne said: haven't got the foggiest love. They continued sitting whilst Nathan searched the room: under the bed, in the little cupboard by the sink, in the cabinet beside her bed with the stupid swinging western doors, behind the bed, behind the curtains, under their chairs, in Leanne's carrier bag, in the security box on top of the cabinet. They had to be there somewhere, they had to be. He shouted: where the hell have they gone? Leanne stood up and brushed imaginary dust from her legs. They're just shoes, she said, now for Christ sake pull yourself together. He looked under the bed again. Down on his knees. A nurse entered the room and asked if everything was okay. Leanne and Roy assured the nurse that everything was okay. But from under the bed Nathan said: they're not just shoes, they're her way home. The nurse knelt down and with a tilted head asked if he was okay. And he replied that he was fine, just fine. After a short discussion the nurse revealed that a pair of scruffy trainers had been handed into reception earlier in the day by an old lady who feared that the hospital was under the attack of Israeli shoe bombers. That made them all laugh. And a couple of weeks after that the shoes went into a blue holdall and Nathan took the blue holdall everywhere: foot wells of planes, backseats of cars, under the desk, park benches, supermarket trolleys, sofas, cinemas, beaches, the other chair in a restaurant, the other side of the bed.

Chris Edwards-Pritchard is a 25 year old writer living in Gloucestershire, UK. His work has been published in a range of anthologies and magazines, including the prestigious *Bristol Short Story Prize Anthology*, for which he has been shortlisted two years in a row. Some of his work has also recently appeared in the New York journal *Bellevue Literary Review* and, last year, he was delighted to accept the Gregory Maguire Award for Short Fiction in London. You can follow Chris on Twitter: @ChrisEPritchard.

DEBBI VOISEY

Death in the Nest

The bedroom door remained closed all through spring and for most of the summer. When it did open, it was for brief seconds; to let in a man with a fat brown bag made from creaking leather and with scuff marks down the sides, or to bring fresh bedding in and stale, sick smelling bedding out. And endless bowls of soup – full when they went in, and mostly full when they came out.

From her hiding place in the hot press along the landing, through the crack of the almost pulled to door, Marie only ever saw parts of people. Her father's brown corduroy trousers, hanging from his braces over a too big shirt; Mrs Brown's sensible, square-toed shoes and the American Tan tights – thick and heavy looking – that she bought from Connor's on the corner of The Green.

Mrs Brown was what the locals called the street's 'hatcher and despatcher'. Stiff of collar and of back, she had birthed most of the children in the street, and laid pennies on the eyes of countless souls as they left. Fifty years a Garden Street resident and witness to every twist and turn of life.

When he found her hiding in the cupboard, her father took her outside. It had only been nine years since Mrs Brown had held her upside down and smacked her arse and she was too young – he said – to be squashed up in the hot press like some smelly auld sheet.

Outside, the sun cracked the pavement and birdsong punctured the air, along with the blatt and hum of lawnmowers, and her father took her down to the bottom of the garden and pointed up at a nest in the tall maple tree – way, way up.

The sun scorched Marie's skin and her long hair fell into her eyes and she had to swipe it away as she looked up.

Her father told her that the blood and feathers on the grass beneath the tree meant that death had stolen into the nest. The words made her feel slightly giddy. She didn't want to know what had caused the gunk down there on the grass, but he told her that a cat had been here and that they should see how things were, up there in the tree.

He fetched a ladder from his dusty shed; he had to push long stems of grass aside to get through the door. He leaned it up against the maple's trunk, and fragments of bark rained down.

'Hold it still,' he said to her, and she grasped it with chubby hands, watching as his brown corduroy legs moved higher. The sun stung her eyeballs and she had to look away, but she could hear the crackle and rustle of whatever he was doing, and his movements made the ladder vibrate against her palms.

She stared at the grass between her feet, keeping one eye shut because that was where the feathers were; stained red and stuck to the grass.

When at last he came down – carefully, because both his hands were clasped together and he could only use his legs – his eyebrows were raised high and his eyes wide.

'Here, Marie.' He moved his hands forward, towards her. 'Hold out your hands. Close your eyes.'

Her heart beat rapidly, and she felt a little like she did at Christmas when mysterious packages appeared under the tree. But also a little bit like she did when she had to go to the dentist.

But she trusted her father. Implicitly. So, eyes closed and hands shaking like the ladder as her father had climbed, she stretched out her arms. She felt the rough skin of his hands, and he dropped something smooth and wet and wriggling onto her palms and then folded her hands together to make a dome.

'A baby bird,' he told her, and she felt it, trembling in her hands, even before she opened her eyes and saw its tiny beak, its sparse brown feathers against bruise-purple flesh.

In the kitchen, with a glass of pop each, they laid the bird in a shoe box on several layers of kitchen paper. Her father showed her how to feed it water by soaking bits of bread and holding it to its beak, and he fetched some worms from the flower bed and one after one the greedy open mouth in the box swallowed them up.

'Marie.' He stroked her head. 'This little bird lost her ma, but with our love and care, she might just survive. We will do everything we can.'

She didn't understand why his eyes filled with tears, or why he fingered his wedding ring constantly.

The bedroom door continued to open briefly and close for long periods of time. Mrs Brown and the man with the creaking brown bag came and went all through the long, hot weeks. A voice on the radio said the heat wave was set to continue.

Marie opened and closed the lid of the box, watching the scraggy scarecrow of a bird change as the summer passed. Its beak never stopped asking for food, and though she found the slimy, shiny worms gross, she patiently dug them up and dropped them into the hungry mouth.

When he wasn't in the bedroom – when Mrs Brown was 'on duty' - her father helped her. He was the best at finding the worms. Soon, the bird's chirping changed, got louder and stronger.

One Sunday, with bright sun streaming into the kitchen, casting pretty light across the kitchen table and folding the squawking box in a blanket of heat, Mrs Brown came early - dressed in a rigid black dress - and stayed all day.

Marie's father came to her and sat at the table. His braces were dangling at his sides and he wore only a vest – no shirt. His hair stood in sweaty spikes all over his head, and his whiskers cast a shadow over his face.

'It's time,' he said. From upstairs, the sound of a voice, low and rhythmic.

'For what, da?' Marie watched as the box juddered on the table. Tap, tap; like an egg trying to hatch.

'To let go,' he said, and took her hand – and the box from the table – and led her into the garden.

Bees buzzed in the hedge and a sparrow flew by in a wide arc around the house. Her father laughed without humour and said something about the birds and the bees, and how life and death was a circle that sometimes went out of shape.

'This baby lost her ma,' he said, 'but she is going to fly away, strong and healthy, and have babies of her own.'

He opened the box. Fat tears slid down his cheeks and one hit the bird on the top of its head.

Marie watched the bird jump into the air. It was like it had forgotten, or did not know, that it was a bird with wings. Several flaps and a few moments stumbling and falling around the grass like a drunk on his way home, and then suddenly, it was gone.

It flew over the fence, squawking and squeaking, and Marie waved goodbye.

That afternoon, her father propped the bedroom door open, and lots of people went inside. Streams of them, one after the other. Mrs Brown made sandwiches and endless pots of tea.

Across the landing, Marie hid in the hot press, peeping through the crack in the door. She could see into the bedroom: part of the bed, draped in a pale blue quilt; a left arm; a wedding ring just like the one her da had.

She watched as a slat of light from the drawn curtains crept across the room and showered her dead mother with a million motes of golden dust.

Debbi Voisey's first memory of serious writing was penning an episode of her favourite TV programme, Charlie's Angels; sadly not commissioned or seen by any other human! Not a script, but a fan fiction. She's come on a lot since then. She has written three novels and is working on a fourth, but her efforts have been concentrated on one major project for the past few years. She began entering short story competitions a couple of years ago in order to gain some discipline and to learn the art of economy with words! Debbi lives in Stoke-on-Trent with her husband of 26 years, and 'Death in the Nest' is her first longlist success.

JOHN HOLLAND

LIPS

As they were leaving the college she asked him if he wanted a coffee. He said that he only drank tea. And walked on. The following week she asked him if he wanted a tea. In the cafe, they talked about the pottery class. She told him her name was Dorothy. Dorothy, he repeated. He didn't say his name, so she asked. He said it was Ellsworth.

After, he returned to his small room with the skylight and the empty dog basket with the hair-matted maroon rug, and the small circular oak table with the vase shaped stain. And sat in his uncomfortable wooden armed chair, picked up his ballpoint pen and opened his book – the one without the lines – and wrote the date (14 January 2006) and the word 'Tea.'

At the pottery class, he made a black iron glazed stoneware urn which she admired. She made a blue glazed earthenware plate with yellow and white glazed fried eggs, orange glazed beans and brown glazed individually cut chips, which he didn't comment on. After the class she again invited him for a tea. And when classes ceased they continued to meet in the cafe each month. He always drank tea. Occasionally they had a sandwich. Even at those prices.

As they grew more used to each other's company they talked a little less about pottery and a little more about food and about family. Sometimes combining the two. Her mother was as fierce as burnt toast, she said. His sister as silly as a baked bean sandwich.

When he returned to his small room, he would write the date and a word or phrase in his book – the one without the lines. 'Tea' or 'toast' or 'baked beans'

After five teas in five months, they touched cheeks as they parted. His lips briefly on her skin. It felt strange to him. He liked it. He liked her, he thought. He didn't want to do anything sudden. He had done that once before.

Back in his room he placed the metal end of a tape measure against the midpoint of his cheek. Then extended the tape to his lips. The centre, not the edge of his lips. Then removed it, holding the tape between his thumb and forefinger, and examined the numbers and lines on it. One hundred millimetres or ten centimetres. Her cheek and lips must be similar, he thought. Using a blue plastic calculator, a piece of A4 paper from his book – the one with the lines – and a short, almost blunt, pencil, he began to draw up a grid. He calculated that if, when they parted each month, he moved his lips one millimetre towards her mouth he would reach her lips in eight years and four months. He had the time, he thought. He looked in his Oxford Pocket Dictionary, eighth edition, 1992, and wrote the date and the word 'incremental' in his book – the one without the lines. And sighed. Eight years and four months. He didn't want to do anything sudden.

The next time they met (June 2006) he felt slightly anxious, as he had to move his lips one millimetre towards hers. Because of his pre-occupation there was little conversation. Only about pulling handles on jugs and whether he preferred garden or mushy peas. I'm a mushy man, he said. As he parted, he kissed her cheek in what he hoped was one millimetre closer to her lips. He couldn't be exactly sure. He couldn't really measure it, could he? She didn't seem to notice. In his room he wrote the date and the words 'Plan commenced'.

By January 2007 (8 months into his plan) his lips, he thought, had moved roughly eight millimetres towards her lips. He didn't think that she had noticed. He barely had.

When they met in the cafe in March 2007 (10 months/10 mm) he talked about the Japanese potter Hamada, and she talked about her husband. He said that he didn't know she had a husband. Didn't you notice my ring? she asked. No, he said. His name is Chip, she said. Chip, he repeated. Short for Charles, she said. Like on the plate you made? he said. Yes, she laughed. In his room he wrote in his book the date and the word 'Chip'. It made him sad. And a bit hungry.

In May 2007 (one year/12 mm) he asked her if, as well as a husband, she had a dog. No, she said. It's just that I have a basket, he said. Sorry, she said.

In September 2007 (one year 4 months/16 mm) they talked about transfer-printed pottery and she told him that she dyed her hair. What, is it not really green? he asked. No, she said, and called him silly. He had been called silly before. But, for the first time, he liked it. Are your eyes really blue? he asked. Oh yes, although they used to be more blue, she said. When he returned to his room he wrote the date and the words 'Less blue'.

In July 2008 (2 years 2 months/26 mm) she told him that she had left her husband. Why? he asked. I don't like him, she said. Me neither, he said. But you haven't met him, she said. I'm just supposing, he said. She told him she was now living with her sister. Does she have a dog? he asked. No, she said.

In September 2009 (3 years 4 months/40 mm) they talked about glazes, including nuka, the oriental rice-based glaze. She told him she had met an Egyptian sculptor. He had dreadlocks, she said. Dreadlocks – very secure, he said.

In December 2009 (3 years 7 months/43 mm) she told him that the Egyptian sculptor made his work from human faeces and blood. Human faeces and blood, he repeated. When they parted he checked her cheek before kissing it. In his room he wrote the date and the words 'Shit sculptor'.

In May 2010 (4 years/48 mm) she told him she had moved in with the Egyptian sculptor. He blinked and said nothing. Later he said he had a headache and stood and left without kissing her cheek. In his room, he regretted doing that.

In December 2010 (4 years 7 months/55 mm) they talked about kick wheels and she told him she was pregnant. With a baby? he asked. Yes, she said. When he returned to his room he wrote the date and the word 'Baby' in bigger letters than usual.

In June 2011, back in his room, he reviewed his plan. Over five years had elapsed. He believed he had moved his lips slightly more than six centimetres. He thought he was on target. He didn't want to do anything sudden.

In July 2011 Ellsworth didn't see Dorothy, because she was having a baby.

In August 2011 a woman in the laundrette asked him if he would like a coffee. Tea, he said, and felt proud of his assertiveness. In the cafe, he asked her name. Ernestine, she said. Ernestine, he repeated. He chatted to her about clay and throwing and glazes and kilns. She seemed interested. As they parted he moved to kiss her cheek. Instead she kissed his lips. When he returned to his room he wrote the date and the words 'Spin cycle.'

The next month, September 2011, he met Ernestine again. At her suggestion he tried a cappuccino, but didn't enjoy it. He brought with him a copy of Ceramic Review which he lent her. He asked her if she ever threw pots. Only when I'm cross, she said. He didn't get it. He asked her if she was married. No, she said. Whether she dyed her hair. No, she said. Whether she knew anyone who made sculpture from human faeces and blood. No, she said. What's with all the questions? she asked. As they parted she kissed him again on the lips, and asked him if he wanted to see her room. Do you have a dog? he asked. No, sorry, she said. When he got back to his room he wrote the date and the word 'No.' He regretted lending her the Ceramic Review.

In January 2012 (5 years 8 months/68 mm) he met Dorothy again and this time she brought the baby. He asked his name. Donald, she said. Donald, he repeated. He asked if that was an Egyptian name. Not really, she said. When they parted he wasn't sure whether to kiss the baby on the cheek too. He didn't. But he did move his lips seven millimetres nearer her lips to compensate for the period when he hadn't seen her. He hoped that this was not too sudden and that she would not notice. As far as he knew she didn't. Although he thought Donald might have.

In July 2012 (6 years 2 months/74 mm) Donald was with her again and cried and seemed unhappy. She said she had to go and change him. When she came back he was surprised. It's the same baby, he said. He's just pooed, she said. He asked if the baby's poo would be used for a sculpture. She said it wouldn't.

In February 2013 (6 years 9 months/81 mm) she stopped bringing Donald with her. Her mother was looking after him. Is she as fierce as burnt toast with him? he asked. You've got a good memory, she said, but no, she's nice to Donald. They talked about Japanese anagama kilns. And she told him that she'd left the Egyptian sculptor. To come for a coffee? he asked. No, forever, she said. That's a long time, he said. Are you pleased? she asked. Yes, he said. She looked at him. He didn't want to do anything sudden. When he returned to his room he wrote the date and the word 'Forever'.

In December 2013 (7 years 7 months/91 mm) he talked to her about the best time to buy a new dog. How long since your dog died? she asked. He paused. His eyes moved upwards and to the right as he thought. I've never owned a dog, he said. Now might be a good time then, she said. When he returned to his room he wrote the date, and, in a rather shaky hand, the word 'Now'.

Each time they met she asked if he'd bought a dog. He hadn't.

In August 2014 (8 years 3 months/99 mm) he knew he was one millimetre from his target. They talked about the porous qualities of unglazed earthenware. When he returned to his room he wrote the date and the words 'Rome wasn't built in eight years and four months'

In September 2014 (8 years 4 months/100 mm) he knew he had reached his target date. He felt anxious. They talked about salt glazing and its impact on the environment. But he knew what he must ask himself to do. He tried to summon all the courage it had taken to hatch his plan, the courage he'd needed to try that cappuccino, the courage he'd shown by not going to Ernestine's room, the courage that had made him wait so long – so very long – for this woman. When they were about to part, he pressed his lips gently on hers.

That was sudden, she said.

When he returned to his small room with the skylight and the empty dog basket with the hair-matted maroon rug, and the small circular oak table with the vase shaped stain, he sat in his uncomfortable wooden armed chair, and picked up his pen and opened his book –the one without the lines – and wrote the date and the word 'Lips'. And then she wrote the word 'Lips' too.

John Holland wrote topical gags for BBC Radio and *Punch* in the 80s and began writing short fiction in 2011. Competition judges and publishers have been kind, so his work can be found online in magazines and in anthologies including *The Best Stories in a Decade* (2013). He sometimes takes his stories on the road. John is the organiser of Stroud Short Stories, a non-profit-making twice-yearly short story event in Gloucestershire. More about John is to be found on www.johnhollandwrites.com and more about SSS on stroudshortstories.blogspot.co.uk